"I love a challenge,"

Hunter said. "I want to change your mind about us wranglers, Deni."

Their gazes locked, and Deni's heart began to thud against her ribs. Her resistance began to waver.

"Why should I change?" Deni asked stubbornly.

Hunter got to his feet and began to pace the room. "Reason number one: to erase your prejudices about cowboys. A smart woman like you should be way above that sort of foolishness."

He continued before she could comment. "Reason number two: you need some help. I'm free at the moment and can offer my services."

Deni snorted. "I can take care of myself. Any more reasons?"

Hunter rubbed his chin thoughtfully and then gave her a mischievous smile. Deni's eyes widened in alarm when he stalked over to her, a heart-stopping gleam of determination in his eye. He pulled her to her feet, wrapped his arms around her and said, "Reason number three," before he covered her lips with his.

Dear Reader,

Welcome to Silhouette—experience the magic of the wonderful world where two people fall in love. Meet heroines that will make you cheer for their happiness, and heroes (be they the boy next door or a handsome, mysterious stranger) who will win your heart. Silhouette Romance reflects the magic of love—sweeping you away with books that will make you laugh and cry, heartwarming, poignant stories that will move you time and time again.

In the coming months we're publishing romances by many of your all-time favorites, such as Diana Palmer, Brittany Young, Sondra Stanford and Annette Broadrick. Your response to these authors and our other Silhouette Romance authors has served as a touchstone for us, and we're pleased to bring you more books with Silhouette's distinctive medley of charm, wit and—above all—*romance*.

I hope you enjoy this book and the many stories to come. Experience the magic!

Sincerely,

Tara Hughes
Senior Editor
Silhouette Books

LINDA VARNER

Heart
Rustler

Published by Silhouette Books New York
America's Publisher of Contemporary Romance

To my little sister, Pennie Pennington,
who cried with me long-distance
when they killed off Magnum.

To my big sister, Joanne Thompson,
who bought a wineglass for me to toss
in the fireplace when I sold a book ...
just like Joan Wilder.

SILHOUETTE BOOKS
300 E. 42nd St., New York, N.Y. 10017

ISBN: 0-373-08644-X

First Silhouette Books printing Apriil 1989

All the characters in this book are fictitious. Any
resemblance to actual persons, living or dead, is
purely coincidental.

Printed in the U.S.A.

Books by Linda Varner

Silhouette Romance

Heart of the Matter #625
Heart Rustler #644

LINDA VARNER

has always had a vivid imagination. For that reason, while most people counted sheep to get to sleep, she made up romances. The search for a happy ending sometimes took more than one night, and when one story grew to mammoth proportions Linda decided to write it down. The result was her first romance novel.

Happily married to her junior high school sweetheart, the mother of two and a full-time secretary, Linda still finds that the best time to plot her latest project is late at night, when the house is quiet and she can create without interruption. Linda lives in Conway, Arkansas, where she was raised, and believes the support of her family, friends and writers' group made her dream to be published come true.

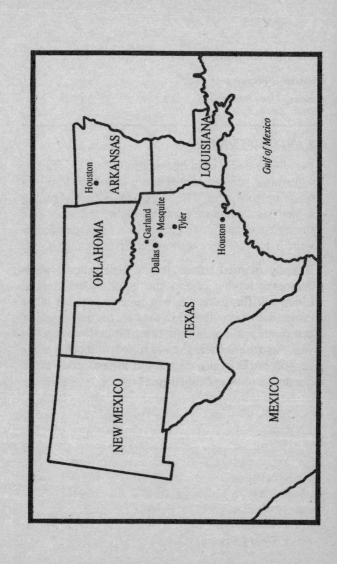

Chapter One

Mister, where I come from, men don't treat women that way."

Deni Hadley's head jerked up at the sound of that dangerous Texas drawl. Her eyes widened in shock, her gaze sweeping over worn leather boots, form-hugging jeans and suede jacket. Glittering brown eyes turned away from her inebriated escort to lock with hers. A hand reached out to pull her up from where she'd fallen at the bottom of the steps outside the restaurant.

"Look, cowboy," Paul Grogan blustered, stepping forward to hamper her would-be rescuer's effort. "Butt out. This is between me and my date."

"You mean she's not your wife?" The tall stranger straightened up slowly, pushing back his sweat-stained cowboy hat. A flicking muscle in his chiseled jaw was the only indication that he might be upset.

"This tramp?" Grogan asked, laughing uproariously. Deni gasped at the insult.

Grogan's laughter became a grunt of pain when the other man punched him in the stomach. His knees buckled and he collapsed—out cold—on the steps down which he had just shoved Deni.

"Oh-my-gosh! You've killed him!" Deni gasped, her life flashing before her eyes. Visions of police officers, jails and scandal assailed her. Panic-stricken, she struggled to get to her feet, hampered by her full skirt. Impatiently she reached up a hand for help. Her handsome savior took it, this time successfully tugging her to her feet.

"Are you all right?" He'd stepped closer and his piercing brown eyes caught the glow of the street lamps overhead.

"Never mind me," Deni told him, oddly flustered by his nearness. "You need to call an ambulance for Paul."

"I really didn't hit him very hard." The cowboy dropped one knee to the pavement so he could take the pulse of the prostrate man. "He's all right—just plastered."

"This is great," Deni muttered, her disgruntled manner belying her words. "What on earth am I going to do with him?"

"Nothing," the cowboy advised, flicking Grogan a cold look.

"But I can't just leave him here on the steps," she argued.

"Why not? With a little luck he'll be so mad he'll never ask you out again."

"Contrary to what he told you, he is *not* my date," she informed him. "This was a business appointment. He promised to introduce me to his boss, a man I'm dying to meet, and though he apparently lied about the whole thing, I can hardly abandon him here in this condition. Now I thank you for your help, Mr...."

"Nash. Hunter Nash." He grinned. "And you are...?"

"Denise Hadley."

"I'll bet your friends call you Neesy," Hunter teased, rather inappropriately, considering Paul lay unconscious at their feet.

"My friends call me Deni," she retorted, impatient to be rid of this too-helpful rodeo bum. That he was a rodeo bum, she never doubted for a moment. Years of training had given her the knack of spotting one a mile away. "Look, Mr. Nash—"

"Hunter."

Deni heaved a sigh. "Look, I appreciate your coming to my rescue, but it really wasn't necessary."

"Wasn't necessary?" he echoed in disbelief. "That jerk just pushed you down a flight of stairs."

"Three steps is hardly a 'flight' and it was an accident. If I hadn't been so close to the edge of the steps, I wouldn't have lost my balance."

"And if there had been seven steps instead of three, you might have broken your neck."

Deni bit back a rejoinder, knowing he was right. Not for the first time that night, she wondered what she was doing out with a jerk like Paul Grogan anyway. Surely there was an easier way to meet the mystery man who owned Heart Rustler women's fashions than through his amorous marketing representative.

"But my neck's just fine and I really can manage from here."

"What are you going to do?"

Good question, Deni acknowledged silently, glancing around. She wasn't familiar with this section of

Dallas. Paul Grogan had suggested they meet at this particular restaurant since she wouldn't agree to let him pick her up at her house. He'd said it was near his office and his favorite bar and that he wanted to unwind before he introduced her to his employer.

Deni grimaced, well aware that Paul's propensity for happy hour should have been her first clue that the evening might not be a total success. Another clue should have been the fact that no one else at the Heart Rustler enterprise—from the receptionist to the office manager—would even *acknowledge* her pleas to meet its reclusive owner.

To her dismay, she found herself near tears. What a difference from her earlier mood of jubilation when she thought she was going to meet the man she hoped to work for someday and possibly even show him some of her clothing designs. The gathering crowd and the realization that she should have had more sense than to get into such a fix in the first place did nothing for her plummeting spirits. Neither did the steadily worsening headache she'd been fighting all day.

Obviously picking up on her blue mood, Hunter reached out, patting her shoulder awkwardly. "Don't get upset, ma'am. I was just trying to understand why you feel obligated to help someone who just tried to murder you."

"Paul Grogan did *not* try to murder me," she protested, dipping her head forward to stretch the aching muscles in the back of her neck.

Holy Moses! Hunter's breath left his lungs in a controlled hiss of surprise. He gave the man at his feet a second, sharper look. So *this* was Paul Grogan, his marketing rep of two months. Hunter was astounded that he hadn't recognized his employee before he'd punched him. Hadn't he left the security of his ranch to discuss this very person with Susan Masterson, his office manager? Hadn't he seen a photograph of the man? But then it was only a poor snapshot, and just now Hunter's eyes had been glued to Deni, not her escort.

Apparently Susan was right. She *had* overheard Grogan agreeing to introduce someone—obviously Deni—to Hunter even though no one at Heart Rustler except Susan and her husband, Chuck, who was head of the Art Department, really knew his identity. Incredible. And what a quirk of fate that they should have chosen one of Hunter's favorite restaurants for the meeting—a restaurant he always visited when he made occasional night visits to his office.

Ever since an innovative advertising campaign had made Heart Rustler clothing the "in" choice of the season, Hunter's Dallas office had been inundated not only with persistent journalists in search of an exposé on the mystery man who owned the company, but with representatives from larger design companies wanting to buy him out. Susan had felt certain that Deni was one or the other because she'd refused to talk to anyone but the "boss." Little did Deni know Hunter didn't intend to reveal his identity to anyone. He also didn't intend to sell out.

Hunter brought himself out of his musings with difficulty, suddenly noting the young woman's pallor. Pesky journalist or whatever, she obviously needed help. "You're as white as a sheet. Are you sure you're all right?"

"I'm fine except for a headache, which I've had all day. It seems to be getting worse."

"And no wonder. Why don't you just let me handle this?"

"Oh, would you?" she asked, obviously relieved. Hunter noted her trembling bottom lip and the lines of strain around her brilliant blue eyes. She looked near the end of her tether—delicate, helpless and incredibly appealing. And even though he knew that Susan was undoubtedly right and Deni was the last kind of person he needed in his life right now, Hunter still felt responsible for her. Sure, she should have seen through Grogan's lies, but she was also a damsel in distress and pretty as all get-out. What southern male could resist such a combination?

"Even though I think we ought to leave him here," Hunter told her, "I'll help you. Now where does he live?"

Deni tried to concentrate on the question, but it wasn't easy. She felt slightly dizzy and swayed, jumping when Hunter's hands unexpectedly slid behind her back, pulling her close to support her. Too aware of her suddenly pounding heart and his warm breath fanning her hair, she said, "I don't know, and please let go of me."

"Yes, ma'am." Hunter released her so abruptly she wobbled. She noted that he almost reached for her again, but put his hands into his pockets instead. "Does he have a car?"

"I don't know."

"Is there someone we should call?"

"I don't know," she admitted yet again.

Hunter rolled his eyes heavenward and snorted with impatience. "What, exactly, do you know?"

Deni blinked once to clear her migraine-blurred vision, and said, "I know if I don't get off my feet pretty soon I'm going to faint, that's what I know."

"That does it," Hunter told her, stepping over the legs of his recently hired, and of this moment fired, employee. He put an arm around Deni's waist. "Would you go inside and get some help for this man?" he asked one of the gawking bystanders with a terse nod in the unconscious man's direction. As soon as someone left to do his bidding, he requisitioned someone else to keep an eye on Grogan until help arrived. Then he looked down at Deni, who'd rested her head on his shoulder for a moment and closed her eyes. "There, your feller's all taken care of. Now why don't I drive you home?"

"No thanks, and he's *not* my fellow," Deni snapped, easing away. She smoothed down her dress, a beautiful garment with a slight western flair, and reached down to retrieve her purse. "This meeting was strictly business, and if he hadn't indulged in happy hour, he would probably have been a fairly decent companion." She drew a deep breath and stuck out her right hand, which trembled noticeably. "You've been very kind, Hunter. I won't impose on you further—"

"It was no imposition," he assured her, taking her hand as he added, "and I really think I should drive you home."

"That won't be necessary," she told him, easing her fingers free of his.

Hunter glanced toward the restaurant's parking lot a few yards away. "Is your car close by?"

"Yes," she answered, for the first time taking a really close look at her cowboy. Her eyes didn't limit their inspection to his face, but rather slid down over his muscular neck to a glimpse of golden-bronze chest, which was revealed by his partially unbuttoned shirt. A few dark, curly hairs peeked out, enticing her to touch. She caught her breath, surprised by her errant thoughts, and dragged her gaze back up.

"Then I'll walk you."

"There's no need," she assured him hastily, now more than a little eager to get away from him. He was so close she could smell his tantalizingly spicy aftershave. Deni marveled at her breathless reaction to the sheer maleness of him. It had been a long time since any man had affected her like this. But then, she'd been carefully avoiding cowboys for years now. "I can manage."

"All right then, ma'am," he agreed, much to her relief. "You're on your own."

"Thanks," she said, adding awkwardly, "for everything."

He didn't respond for a moment, eyes narrowed, face solemn. Then he murmured, "Don't mention it."

Acutely conscious of his steady gaze, Deni turned to make her way across the parking lot to her car. She spotted it almost instantly and smiled in relief. It was a beautiful car—new, a gorgeous shade of red and all hers.

With pleasure Deni ran her hand lightly over the gleaming metal fender as she walked to the door. She opened her oversized purse, reaching inside to grope for her always-elusive keys. When she didn't locate them right away, she shook the purse, waiting for the telltale jingle that would tell her in what corner they were tucked. There was no jingle.

Deni checked the deep pockets of the dress she'd designed herself and then, sighing her exasperation, knelt down, dumping the contents of her purse on the asphalt at her feet.

"Something wrong?"

Deni didn't even need to look up to know who'd asked that question. Haphazardly she rifled through the sundry items laying at her feet. "I seem to have misplaced my keys."

"Are they in a blue leather case?"

"Yes!" she exclaimed excitedly. "Do you see them?"

"Uh-huh."

Deni looked up then, her eyes following the direction of Hunter's gaze. Heart sinking, she got to her feet, immediately spotting the keys, safe in the ignition of her locked car. Well *darn*. She'd never done such a thing before and realized she must have been more rattled about this meeting tonight than she'd realized.

She turned slightly, sagging against the car door, her face so forlorn that Hunter's heart went out to her in spite of his disgust for her probable occupation. "This is a hardtop," he said. "I might be able to maneuver a coat hanger inside to unlock the door."

"And risk scratching it?" she responded, horrified.

"New?"

"Brand spanking," she qualified, firmly adding, "no coat hanger."

"I don't suppose you have a spare set of keys?" he asked softly.

"Sure I do," she told him. "At home in a drawer."

Hunter controlled his threatening smile with difficulty, strangely pleased with this latest development and pretty sure he knew why. He was extremely curious about Deni Hadley and oddly touched by the sincerity of her concern for a jerk like Grogan. He decided that he wanted to know more about her.

"I suppose I could call a locksmith," she mused, nervously tossing her straight, golden-brown hair back over her shoulder. It looked silky soft to Hunter and he resisted an urge to reach out to test the accuracy of his guess. A feathery layer of bangs framed her delicate oval face. Her upturned nose was lightly freckled, her cheeks flushed from agitation. To Hunter's discerning eye, she was breathtakingly beautiful, *and*, he ruthlessly reminded himself, out to get him.

"And one would come for fifty dollars," he replied with a solemn nod, more than a little disconcerted by the direction his thoughts had taken.

"Fifty dollars!" she exploded. "That's outrageous."

"I agree," he said. Anxious to get on with this rescue so he could return to the safety of his ranch, he then suggested, "Why don't you just give in and let me take you home? I really don't mind."

But *I* do, Deni thought. Hunter Nash was darned attractive and tempted as she was to let herself take advantage of his offer to help, she had to remember he was a cowboy. And she had a documented weakness for them.

"I can't let you do that," she told him.

"Sure you can," he answered. "My truck's right over there. Let me help you get your things together." He bent down, randomly cramming everything back into her purse. After hesitating a moment, she knelt down to help.

It was late, her head hurt and she *didn't* have fifty dollars to spare. Hunter Nash had come to her rescue once already this night. Surely it wouldn't hurt to let him help again. Then they would say goodbye and both get on with their separate lives. On that encouraging thought, she snapped her bag shut. Together they walked the short distance to a badly dented, mud-caked, pickup truck.

Hunter opened the door on the passenger side and stepped back so she could get in. For the first time in his thirty-two years, he actually wished he had a more classy vehicle like a Ferrari or a Porsche instead of this twelve-year-old eyesore, and that realization gave him pause.

Why did he care what some misguided woman thought of him? he wondered. He wasn't trying to impress anyone—least of all Deni Hadley. And though everything about her, from her big blue eyes to the vaguely familiar scent of her cologne intrigued him, he had no intention of risking his precious anonymity to get to know her better. She was trouble—big trouble. He'd do well to get her home and out of his life as quickly as possible.

Deni glanced at Hunter before she got into the truck, giving his face one last, thoughtful perusal. Just why was he being so nice? she wondered. Was that gleam in his eye more than reflection? Suddenly assailed by second thoughts, she doubted her wisdom in letting this distressingly appealing stranger drive her home.

Home? No way. Deni Hadley may have made an error in judgment once already tonight, but she wasn't a total fool. She had no intention of being alone with this devastating cowboy one minute longer than necessary. Her Garland, Texas, home was nearly twenty miles away. Surely there was somewhere closer he could take her.

"I have an apartment near here," she impulsively told him, naming the area where her cousin, Seth, lived, courtesy of his well-to-do parents. She hoped Seth would be home and could convince her champion she would survive if he exited her life as abruptly as he had entered it.

"I'm familiar with the area." He headed around the front of the truck to the driver's side. While he did that, she grabbed the opportunity to inspect her surroundings. The floor beneath her feet was covered in clumps of dried dirt, hay and heaven only knew what else. Not surprisingly, a colorful pouch of chewing tobacco lay on the dash. Deni shuddered.

Hunter got into the truck beside her and shut the door. When he inserted the key into the ignition and turned it, the radio blasted the soulful refrain of a current country-and-western hit. Deni shuddered again.

Wearily she leaned her head against the window and shut her eyes, marveling at how much this male appealed to her physically in spite of his life-style. Apparently she had no resistance to—or sense regarding—men in cowboy hats.

Just let me get home, she prayed. *I'll never have to see this goat roper again. I can get on with my quest for Mr.-Perfect-in-a-three-piece-suit.*

At that moment he pulled out of the lot, driving under a streetlight, which for one brief instant illuminated his ruggedly handsome face. Deni's heart did a flip-flop.

"Do you like living in Dallas?" Hunter asked after they'd driven several blocks.

"Dallas is a beautiful city," she said.

"Yeah, it is," he agreed. "And I enjoy my trips to town, but that doesn't mean I'd ever want to live here. I have a ranch in the country, myself."

Ranch? Deni flicked him a disdainful glance. How typically Texan, she thought, to call every two-bit farm a "ranch." She could just picture his spread—dirt road, white frame house, chickens dotting the yard, maybe even a pig or two. Some unpleasant memories surfaced and she grimaced just as they drove under a streetlight. Hunter caught that expression.

"What's the matter?"

"Nothing," she lied, allowing herself another quick peek at him. It didn't help. "Ranch" or not, he still looked good enough to kidnap, darn him. Deni was vastly irritated by her reaction to Hunter and unconsciously ventilated some of her ire when she snapped, "Is your *ranch* near Dallas, then?"

"Near enough," he replied tersely. Her derogatory tone angered him. So she was a snob on top of everything else. She had no use for redneck cowboys, fresh from the barn. What would she say if she knew this particular one was the man she'd gone to such incredible trouble to meet? How he would have loved to reveal his true identity, put this woman in her place once and for all. He was proud of his country roots. His paternal grandparents had been farmers and he cherished his memories of the happy hours spent in their home.

Now I've hurt his feelings, Deni thought, detecting a bit of temper in his answer. He'd been nothing but nice to her, and he certainly didn't deserve her misdirected wrath. Was it his fault he was so darned appealing? Reaching out, she tugged his jacket sleeve. "I'm sure your ranch is lovely."

"I like it," he told her, some of his irritation fading. She was, after all, a city slicker. One had to make allowances for such. He took a deep breath, forcing himself to relax, and said, "It's not far to *your* place now." Then he smiled.

And what a smile. Deni moaned silently when she caught a glimpse of the dazzling expression that softened his rugged features into irresistible boyishness. She knew at once that if this bronc-busting, cattle-roping male was even a fourth as attracted to her as she was to him, she wouldn't have a prayer. Somehow she had to ensure she never, *ever* saw him again under any circumstances.

"My husband, Seth, will be glad you're going to this trouble," Deni said, suddenly inspired. "He's a lot like you—thinks I can't take care of myself."

"I thought you said you weren't married," Hunter responded, frowning.

"I said *Paul* and I weren't married," she corrected, hiding her satisfied smile. That should do it. If he was at all interested, and she couldn't really be sure of that, he now thought she was married. Good. She managed what she hoped was an innocent smile, holding that unnatural expression until the headlights of an oncoming car revealed it to her companion.

"I see."

She certainly hoped he did. The rest of the short trip was completed in silence. When Hunter pulled into Seth's street, Deni glanced at her watch—nine o'clock. If he wasn't home, she wouldn't be able to get inside the apartment. Then what would she do?

To Deni's relief, Seth's '57 Chevy was in his driveway. Hunter parked his truck behind it and said, "It's as black as pitch out here. I'll walk you to the door."

"You can't do that," Deni protested, imagining what Seth's reaction would be.

"Why not?" he asked. "Is your husband the jealous type?"

"Oh, no," Deni thoughtlessly assured him. "He doesn't have a jealous bone in his body." Now why had she said that?

Hunter muttered something that sounded like, "...must be crazy..." and got out of the vehicle.

Sighing in resignation, Deni did the same. In moments they were on the unlit porch. Deni fumbled for the doorbell even as Hunter commented, "Seems like he could have left the light on for you."

Deni dared not reply to that. They stood outside for what seemed an eternity before she saw a silhouette on the frosted oval glass on the wooden door. She sagged with relief, sending a prayer heavenward that her ordeal was almost over. A second later, Seth opened the door. Loud music assaulted their ears and Deni cringed, glancing uneasily at Hunter.

"Denise!" Seth exclaimed, smiling broadly. "What are you doing in this neck of the woods?"

Uh-oh. Deni swallowed hard, giving her favorite cousin an exaggerated wink. "You're such a comedian, Seth," she scolded, her eyes sweeping his familiar, lanky form. She was so glad to see him, even under these extenuating circumstances. It had been several weeks since their last contact—she'd been busy in her dress shop, he'd been caught up in the first few months of his freshman year at the university. Normally she saw him at least once every week. He was her home away from home, someone warm and familiar to cling to when life got too confusing.

But right now he didn't look so familiar. Dressed in a threadbare half T-shirt, tight blue jeans—without knees—and tattered running shoes, he could have been any one of the hundreds of college students who lived in the area. His hair was shaggier than she'd ever seen it and looked badly in need of combing. What a change from the meticulous future farmer with whom she'd grown up.

"I locked my keys in the car. This gentleman was kind enough to help me home." She stressed the last word, hoping he would play along without question. At this point she couldn't be too sure, for he stared at her wordlessly. "You *are* going to let us in, aren't you, *darling*?"

Abruptly Seth came to life. "Uh, sure. Come in." He stepped back to allow them enough room to enter the apartment. With long-legged strides, Seth led the way to the tiny living room where a girl sat on the couch, lost in the beat of the music. When she finally realized she wasn't alone, she flicked a glance at the three, winked at Seth and tossed back her crimped hair. Awed, Deni looked questioningly at Seth, who shrugged sheepishly.

A girlfriend, she thought, her heart sinking. That possibility hadn't even occurred to her. Her eyes locked with Hunter's. She noted the strange expression on his face. Disbelief? she wondered. Well maybe, but not just that. Disgust? That was more like it.

What could only be garbage littered the stained carpet under their feet. A month's worth of laundry decorated every chair and table, as did several cowboy hats in various stages of wear and tear. She grimaced with embarrassment, wondering what Hunter thought of her housekeeping. *Her housekeeping?* Of course not. Deni kept a perfect house, but he would never know that.

"Thanks, Mr. Nash," she said brightly, choosing not to try to explain the presence of the other female in the room. Seth and Hunter eyed each other warily and "Girlfriend" now watched with unabashed curiosity, her contortions reduced to a seductive wiggle. "We won't keep you any longer."

Hunter ignored her open invitation to leave, instead sticking out his hand and introducing himself to her cousin. "Hunter Nash."

"Seth Hadley."

"Your wife had a fall, Mr. Hadley," Hunter said, taking off his hat. His finger combed his thick dark hair.

"What happened?" Seth demanded, thankfully not reacting to the news that his cousin was now his wife. "Girlfriend's" shadowed eyes narrowed in suspicion, however.

"The man I met tonight had too much to drink," Deni interjected. "He got a little rough."

Seth raised an eyebrow. "Oh? And Mr. Nash, here, rescued you?"

"Yes, he did," Deni said, deliberately not explaining just how that had been accomplished. A malicious twinkle in Seth's eyes suddenly brought to mind his mean teasing streak. It seemed the same old Seth lurked just behind the typical-student facade after all. Deni felt a moment of real panic.

"Why don't you just thank Mr. Nash and let him go. I'm sure he's sick of Denise Hadley and her problems."

Seth glanced at Hunter and grinned wickedly. "What'd you do to him, Nash?"

Hunter shrugged. "It was the liquor that got him as much as my blow."

Seth howled with laughter. "Punched him out, did you? Sorry I missed it." He glanced at Deni, clearly enjoying the idea of her being involved in a scene of any kind—and especially with a cowboy. "Sounds like you had an interesting evening, sugar. Tell me about this guy you were meeting."

Deni caught her breath, not missing the sharp look Hunter shot her way. "Really, Seth," she said with a nervous laugh. "Don't you ever listen to anything I say?'' She smiled at Hunter. "My husband will show you to the door, Mr. Nash. Thanks again for everything."

"This way," Seth said good-naturedly, leaving the room.

Hunter, however, didn't follow immediately. He just stood there, clearly unwilling to leave Deni with these two, even if one of them were her spouse. There was a long, uncomfortable silence as he perused the room, "Girlfriend" and finally, Deni. He looked decidedly puzzled.

She gave him an encouraging nod, and after a heart-stopping hesitation, Hunter turned to follow Seth outside. The young woman on the couch, motionless for the moment, looked openly hostile. Deni gave her a weak smile, wondering if she were capable of physical violence. Warily, she leaned back in the chair, her eye on her adversary as she tried to relax. Everything was going to be all right. Seth had come through and she wasn't going to have a chance to make a fool of herself over another cowboy.

Hunter walked out the front door to face Deni's husband. He took in Seth's torn shirt, ragged-to-the-point-of-indecency jeans and stringy hair. Seth looked young. Very young. Too young. Like Deni's actions earlier that night, something didn't ring true here. Hunter intended to find out what it was.

"Have you two been married long?" he asked bluntly, wondering how a woman as immaculately dressed as Deni could be married to a sloppy kid like this.

Seth rubbed his chin thoughtfully. His blue eyes twinkled as he made a show of calculating on his fingers the days, months or years involved. Then he glanced at his watch and with a slow smile admitted, "About seven and a half minutes."

Chapter Two

Nearly two hours later, Hunter pulled into the driveway of his sprawling rock-and-cedar ranch just outside Mesquite, a suburb of Dallas. He brought his truck to a screeching halt, which reminded him he needed new brake pads, and climbed out, whistling a merry tune and grinning at his aunt and housekeeper, Hattie Morris. She stood on the porch, hands on ample hips, glaring at him.

"Where've you been?" she demanded. "I've called every friend of yours I could think of—"

"And I wasn't with any of them," Hunter responded, giving her a hug that nearly knocked her down.

"You smell like jasmine, Hunter Nash," she scolded, pushing him away. She tried not to smile, but failed miserably. "Have you got a new girlfriend?"

"Jasmine! *That's* what it is!" he exclaimed, ignoring her question. He brushed past her and entered the split-level structure. His thudding footfall on the gleaming parquet floor echoed in the vast entrance-way.

"Answer me," Hattie said, following him. Hunter turned, tossing his hat toward the hat rack, where it landed unerringly. He grinned at his aunt.

"Why were you looking for me?"

Hattie sighed and gave up gracefully, as she usually did when he refused to let her pry into his affairs. "Lacy called. Said your stepdad had disappeared again. He's been gone three days this time."

Hunter's good mood vanished as it did every time his half sister called with such news. "Dammit, why'd she wait so long to call? Is she staying by herself?"

"Now don't get excited. She's staying with the Stones at night."

"Well, I'm going to get her right now. I told her if Roy pulled this stunt again she was moving in with me, and I meant it."

"It's too late to drive to Tyler tonight, and besides, you can't uproot her in her senior year. She graduates in a few more months. Then you can enroll her in the university just like you planned." When Hunter hesitated, she added, "I know it's rough on you letting her take care of that father of hers, but it's not your place to take over her life. And he loves her, you know."

"Hmph!" Hunter snorted. "He has a funny way of showing it if he does."

"He's just no good, that's all," Hattie commented. "What your poor departed mother ever saw in that man, I'll never know. He caused her nothing but grief and destroyed the wonderful relationship she had with you."

"Roy didn't destroy our relationship. She did that all by herself," Hunter replied, striding into his paneled study, Hattie one step behind. His boots sank into the plush, earth-tone carpet as he made his way to the phone. He dropped into the corduroy recliner and punched out the number his aunt gave him. Hattie perched on the edging of the matching love seat to listen unabashedly.

"Lacy? Hunter here," he said when his younger sister answered the phone. "What's up?"

"*Finally* you're home. It's after eleven and I've been waiting forever for you to call," Lacy scolded.

"Sorry. I had a meeting with Susan tonight. Now tell me what's wrong."

"It's Dad," she responded, a catch in her voice. "I'm really worried about him. He's been gone three whole days. He might be sick—in trouble."

"Most likely he's shacked up somewhere with one of his—" Hunter caught himself in time, remembering he was speaking to a minor. "What I mean is..."

Lacy, the person Hunter cherished most in the world, began to cry because of his harsh rejoinder, and his heart melted instantly. He sighed, knowing he could never hurt his little sister. No matter what his mother's worthless mate cost him in dollars and grief, he would always come to his rescue—for Lacy's sake. She loved that old man and Hunter loved her.

"Don't cry," he soothed. "I'm sorry I said that. I'm upset—worried about you. Are you doing okay?"

"Of course I am. I'm seventeen years old, after all. I can take care of myself," she sniffed, sounding injured.

Hunter heard the censure in her tone and sighed, knowing she could, indeed, take care of herself. She'd been doing exactly that since their mother died four years ago. "I'll do what I can for him, Lacy."

"Oh, thank you. I swear someday I'll make all this up to you."

"I'd rather you came to live with me," Hunter urged.

"Don't start that again. You know I have just seven months of school left. I can't transfer now and besides, Dad needs me."

"Yeah, yeah," Hunter responded impatiently, not up to that familiar argument. "I'll call the sheriff and see what he suggests. I can't imagine what you or I could do that he can't."

"I guess you're right," she agreed. He could hear the relief in her voice and was glad his promise to act had lightened her mood.

"Are you sure you'll be all right at the Stones'?"

"I'll be fine."

"Then I'll call you when I find out something. It may be tomorrow."

"Thanks, bro," she crooned.

Hunter hung up the phone and sat in silence for a moment, staring at nothing. Why? Why? Why? he agonized for the millionth time. Why had his mother married a no-good like Roy Beecher? Why had she felt the need to make a choice between her teenage son and her husband? As the familiar hurt washed over him, Hunter rubbed his eyes, determinedly suppressing his distressing memories.

"Here."

He looked up at his aunt, smiling gratefully and taking the cold beer Hattie handed him. "Where's Uncle Cole?" he asked, before popping the top and drinking half of the icy beverage in one long swallow.

"At home in front of the television. Do you need him?" Hattie asked. She glanced out the window toward the ranch next door.

"Naw. I was just going to give him his tobacco. He left it in the truck today. Thought he might be looking for it."

Hattie wrinkled her nose. "Burn it," she advised, turning on her heel and waving airily as she went out the door.

Hunter laughed and gulped down the rest of the beer. He set down the empty can, leaned back in the chair and closed his eyes for a moment, resting. It had been a trying day, full of problems...and mysteries. Was Grogan the leak at Heart Rustler? he wondered tiredly. Could he expect airtight security now that the man would no longer be there?

And what about Deni? According to Seth, who'd turned out to be a cousin instead of a spouse, Hunter could eliminate reporter as a possible occupation for her. In fact, Seth had found that assumption so hilarious he'd howled with laughter, and that had brought Deni running. She'd monitored the rest of their conversation and, as a result, Hunter hadn't been able to find out anything more.

Now extremely curious about why she'd wanted to talk with him, Hunter knew he wouldn't get a moment's rest until he called that cousin of hers and pumped him for some answers. Hopefully he would cooperate. But first he had another call to make, he reminded himself, sitting forward in the chair and reaching for the phone. It was time to get on with the business of rescuing dear old Roy...again.

Mmm. Coffee.

Deni's eyes opened. She winced against the early

morning light streaming through her windows and then sniffed the air appreciatively. Thank goodness old habits had prevailed and she'd set the timer on the coffee maker last night before falling into bed.

Deni smiled, stretching lazily, and closed her eyes again. She deliberately held at bay her memories of the night before. When she'd finally crawled between the sheets, she had been too tired to analyze what had happened. Now she didn't want to.

Clearly her big dreams of meeting the owner of Heart Rustler and wowing him with her sketch pad had hit a slight snag. Once more it was back to selling dresses instead of designing them, but only for a while. She had to try again since her only option was to prepare what would be a sadly lacking résumé. And who would hire a woman with nothing but a college minor in art and a head full of ideas? No. Deni had to meet this man face-to-face and make him listen to her. They were kindred spirits; he just didn't know it yet.

Deni sighed and snuggled deeper under the covers. The early November breeze stirring the eyelet curtains felt decidedly chilly, heralding the approach of winter. She would have to wear a jacket when Seth came to take her to her car.

Bless Seth's heart, she thought, smiling. He was such a sweetie when he wanted to be. Why, last night he'd buffered the caustic tongue of "Girlfriend," driven Deni home and seen her safely to bed. He hadn't asked a single question—a fact Deni found incredible in light of his family-famous curiosity—and had actually seemed to take in stride her crazy claim they were married, not to mention Hunter's rescue.

Hunter. Unbidden, visions of her champion's sexy smile filled her head and her heart. What a shame he was a wrangler. She could have gone for him in a big way. In the short time Deni had been with Hunter, she'd observed several personality traits she admired, not the least of which were kindness and responsibility. Hadn't he played rescuer even though he didn't know her? Hadn't he done what he could for Paul even though he didn't know him either?

Deni wondered just where Paul Grogan had wound up, not that she really cared. She didn't even know why she'd insisted that Hunter try to help the man; he hadn't deserved any consideration. Imagine Paul thinking she would sleep with him! Deni might want to break into dress design, but not that way. She frowned, remembering Paul's distressing revelation that his employer wouldn't be joining them and why. If Paul's boss really *hadn't* made himself known to his own employees, what chance did the new owner of a tiny dress shop in Garland, Texas, have to meet him? Probably not much. She definitely needed a better plan; she intended to come up with one.

Deni shivered in the brisk air, wishing she'd slept in flannel instead of her cotton, ballerina-length gown. But she loved the dainty garment with its scooped neck, button-up front and old-fashioned charm. In fact, Deni loved anything with an antique flavor. She looked with pride at the four-poster bed that used to be her grandmother's. The eyelet dust ruffle and handmade quilt now adorning it had been picked with care after searching for months for just the right touch.

The cheval mirror and chiffonier had been selected with the same deliberateness. Everything in the room from the braided rugs on the polished wood floors to the pictures on the papered walls bespoke another century.

Deni sighed lustily and glanced at the clock beside her bed. Seven. Time to get up to take the shower she'd been too tired to manage the night before. Seth was coming by at seven-thirty, which was mighty early for him to be up on a Saturday morning, but he'd said he had plans for the rest of the day.

Luckily, Deni's day was free. Since she had a reliable young woman helping out in her dress shop on the weekends, she was deliciously free today and intended to do whatever struck her fancy.

By the time she stepped out of the shower, Deni was wide awake. All she needed to make her a functional human being was a cup of that wonderful-smelling coffee that was waiting in the kitchen. Deni slipped into jeans and a bright red sweater and made a beeline in that direction.

She'd been at the table about fifteen minutes, a mug of the dark brew in one hand and a newspaper in the other, when she heard a knock at the back door.

"Come in," she called out, glancing over her shoulder to double-check that she'd unlocked the door for her cousin.

But it wasn't her cousin who stepped into her kitchen, shutting the door behind him. It was Hunter Nash, and looking for all the world like the stuff of which dreams were made. His softly faded jeans fit like a second skin, accentuating his long legs and muscular thighs. A pale blue western shirt hugged his broad shoulders and chest. Although she wouldn't have believed it possible, he looked even better than she remembered...darn the man. Deni leaped to her feet. "What are you doing here?"

"You told me to come in," he replied. He didn't walk into the room, but remained lounging negligently against the door.

"I thought you were my cous—I mean my husband," she retorted, face flushing.

Hunter grinned at her slip of the tongue. "Jig's up. Seth confessed all."

Deni caught her breath. "What'd he tell you?"

"Let's see..." Hunter mused, eyes twinkling mischievously. "He said you were his cousin and that you were originally from Houston, which didn't surprise me. I'd already decided you were city bred."

She almost choked. Little did Hunter know that Seth meant Houston, Arkansas, a town with a population of less than two hundred. She didn't enlighten him, either. She'd endured years of relentless teasing by friends before she'd managed to shake off the dust of the farm where she'd been raised and was able to acquire her present city look. She wouldn't blow it now. "What else did he say?" she asked.

"Not that much actually."

"And it's a good thing, too," Deni murmured. Hunter chuckled at that—a warm, rumbly sound that further flustered her.

Be strong, she silently beseeched her muddled gray matter. To her dismay, Hunter closed the distance between them, crossing the room to stand beside her.

"Why are you here?" she asked, mortified to hear a tremor in her voice.

"I came to take you to your car," he told her. "And to solve a few mysteries."

"Seth's taking me to my car," Deni answered, tipping her head back so she could meet his steady gaze. "And what mysteries are you talking about?"

"Why you lied about being married, for starters."

"You're a clever man. Figure it out."

"All right." Hunter pulled out one of the cane-back chairs, turned it backward and straddled it. He crossed his arms over the back and rested his chin on them, looking for all the world like a man prepared to stay as long as it took.

"I didn't mean here," Deni hastily told him.

"Why not? What are you afraid of?" His dark eyes glowed. His sexy, I'm-gonna-getcha smile took her breath away. She sank into the chair across from him to keep from falling, knowing exactly what she was afraid of: his lips, his hands, her weakness....

"Nothing," she whispered.

"Then I'll proceed." He sat in silence for a moment, rubbing his chin, deep in thought. "Now why do women usually lie about their marital status?" he mused aloud, almost immediately snapping his fingers even as his face lit up. "I've got it. You're an old maid and don't want anyone to feel sorry for you."

"I *am* not!" Deni blurted out, not at all amused. "Although I'm presently unattached, I *have* been married."

"Presently unattached?"

Deni blushed at her thoughtless admission, nodding self-consciously.

Hunter briefly flashed that smile of his. "Good." Then his face sobered and he frowned, thinking hard once more. "I know!" he exploded seconds later. "You're hopelessly attracted to me and afraid you might not be able to control your raging passion."

Deni gasped at the accuracy of his teasing guess and, with difficulty, regained her shattered composure just enough to snap, "Don't you just wish?"

"As a matter of fact—"

"Why are you here?" Deni asked again, abruptly changing the subject.

"To take you to your car," Hunter repeated.

"Then I'm afraid you've wasted a trip. Seth's doing the honors. Now, I really hate to be rude after all you did for me last night, but goodbye, Hunter."

He gaped at her. "Just goodbye? Is that all the thanks I get for saving you from the big bad wolf and then going back to save the big bad wolf? I'll have you know I found your boyfriend in the bar when I went back to see what had become of him, and I drove him clear across town to the waiting arms of his adoring wife and three small children. It was all I could do not to tell that poor woman what her husband had been up to."

"He's not my boyfriend! I told you last night I only agreed to have dinner with him so I could make a critical contact."

"Oh, yeah, you did mention that. Just who is this person you were risking life and limb to meet?"

His skeptical tone put Deni on the defensive as did the hint of a twinkle in his eye. "No one you'd know, I can promise you that," she replied. To her irritation, Hunter actually laughed. "What's so funny?"

"I was just remembering the look on your face when Grogan invited you to go with him to the 'No Tell Motel.'"

Deni caught her breath. "You heard that?"

Hunter struggled with a smile and nodded.

Deni's face burned. "I didn't deserve his proposition, you know. I was only trying to show my dress designs to his boss. I really thought Paul was going to help me out."

"You design dresses for a living?"

"No, I *sell* them for a living," she corrected, adding, "in my dress shop downtown. So far I haven't been able to get anywhere with my designs."

"And Grogan was supposed to introduce you to someone who could help?"

She sighed. "He said he could—he talked a good game, too."

"Of course he did. He's a salesman."

"How'd you know that?" Deni demanded.

"He told me," Hunter hedged, his curiosity finally appeased somewhat. She was a designer, not a representative of the competition. No doubt she hoped to sell to Heart Rustler. One more mystery solved. Now he could reveal his identity and get on with getting to know her better. Or could he? He was intensely attracted to Deni and hoped the desire he imagined he saw in her eyes was real. If he told her who he *really* was, how could he ever be sure of her motives?

Hunter realized the answer to his dilemma probably lay in the last, unsolved mystery. Last night on the phone, Seth had told him she disliked cowboys. Hunter figured if he could get her to go out with him—a cowboy—tonight, before she knew of his association with Heart Rustler, he could be sure of her. "About Seth coming to take you to your car.... Actually he and I worked out a little switch."

"Seth's not coming?" Deni blurted out, aghast.

"No."

"That rat. He lied to me."

"No he didn't. He was going to come, but I bribed him not to."

"When?"

"Last night on the phone. I called him when I got back to my ranch."

"What'd you bribe him with?" Deni asked, unable to believe Seth would really betray her.

"Two tickets to see Dwight Yoakam in concert next week."

Deni groaned. How diabolically clever Hunter Nash must be. "I can't believe he sold out his own flesh and blood to go hear some cowboy sing."

"And speaking of cowboys, that reminds me of the last mystery I want solved," Hunter said. "But first, would you share your coffee with me?"

Grudgingly Deni got to her feet, skirting the table to walk to one of the oak cabinets. She reached up, extracted a colorful mug and then filled it with coffee. Wordlessly she handed it to Hunter.

"Thanks," he said. He took a sip and grimaced. "Any sugar?"

Deni handed him a spoon and a canister.

"Now any cream?" he asked.

Sighing heavily, she reached into the refrigerator and retrieved a carton, handing it to him. Hunter added generous helpings of both into his cup, took a sip and sighed his pleasure. "Thanks. I needed that. Now, to get on with my detective work. What do you have against cowboys?"

Deni, who'd finally sat back down and taken a sip of her own drink, nearly choked. "What are you talking about?"

"Seth was very surprised you'd even gotten into my truck last night. Said you usually avoided men in cowboy hats."

Darn that Seth and his big mouth. "I do," she admitted.

"Why? What do you have against cowboy hats?"

"Not the hats," Deni replied. "The beer-guzzling, tobacco-chewing men who wear them."

"Do I detect a note of sarcasm here?"

"It's quite possible," she said.

"Did it ever occur to you that looks might be deceiving, Deni?"

"No, my opinions are based on personal observation and years of experience."

"I see. And you'd never even *consider* dating a cowboy?"

"I most certainly would not," she said, shaking her head sharply to emphasize her words.

"So there's no point in me asking you out to dinner tonight?"

"None at all," she assured him.

"Damn, I love a challenge! I want to change your mind about wranglers, Deni."

Their gazes locked. Deni's heart began to thud against her ribs. Her resistance began to waver alarmingly and the idea of having her mind changed began to have a certain amount of appeal.

"You couldn't possibly," she informed him hastily.

"Are you so very sure of that? Sure enough to let me give it a shot?" he persisted.

"Why should I?" Deni asked. She noted how his dark eyes glowed, how his deep dimples added to his appeal, staggering her overcharged senses.

Hunter got to his feet and began to pace the room, his thumbs hooked through his belt loops. He frowned, clearly taking her question seriously. After a long deliberation, he spoke.

"Reason number one: to erase your prejudices against cowboys. A smart woman like you should be way above that sort of foolishness."

"Oh, really?"

"Really. Reason number two: you need some help. I'm free at the moment and can offer my services."

Deni snorted. "I can take care of myself. Any more reasons?"

Hunter rubbed his chin thoughtfully and then gave her a mischievous smile. Deni's eyes widened in alarm when he stalked over to her, a heart-stopping gleam of determination in his eye. He pulled her to her feet, wrapped his arms around her and announced, "Reason number three," before he covered her lips with his.

At first Deni was too stunned to resist him. Then coherent thought became impossible. Whatever the man's faults, he sure could kiss. She had to give him that.

His lips devoured hers. Deni slid her hands over his back and locked them behind his neck in a move that pressed her soft curves against the hard wall of his body.

Hunter growled softly with satisfaction. His mouth left hers to trail across her cheek, unerringly locating the ultrasensitive flesh of her earlobe. Shivers of delight danced up Deni's arms. What was left of her resistance dissolved into a barrage of glorious sensations.

Get a grip! her rational brain screamed. She ignored it, thinking how long it had been since she'd been in this position and how wonderful it felt. Just one more minute, she promised herself. Then she would stop this insanity and send Hunter packing. The minute stretched into two. It was Hunter who finally raised his head, smiling at her. His dark eyes smoldered with desire, further fueling her own.

"I think reason number three is the one," he whispered.

Deni heaved a loud sigh of defeat. She broke free. "I think you're right," she groaned. "And it's the worst reason of all."

"Why do you say that?" he asked, tangling his fingers in her tousled hair. "What's wrong with two people being physically attracted to each other?"

"There's more to a mature relationship than sex. I, for one, want something deeper at this stage of my life."

"I have lots more to offer. Good sex is just an extra, added bonus." He moved toward her again, closing the inches between them.

"Please don't," Deni begged. "You mustn't think that kiss meant anything special or ever will. It was just hormones getting the best of good sense. I don't intend to let you complicate my life. I have goals, plans.... I don't have time for any kind of distraction right now."

"And I'm distracting?" Hunter asked hopefully.

"Mildly," she hedged. "In an amusing sort of way."

Although Hunter didn't actually smile, his dimples deepened and his eyes twinkled. "So you find me amusing?"

"Yes, I do."

"Well, I was hoping for sexy or maybe virile, but I guess amusing beats nothing," he commented, picking up his empty mug and walking over to the counter to refill it. Then he sat down at the table again. "We'll work on those others later."

"Later? Never. Haven't you heard a word I've said? There *is* no later for us."

"Give me three reasons why not," he challenged, propping an elbow on the table. "I did the same for you."

Deni took a deep breath. "All right," she said, getting to her feet to begin some pacing of her own. "Reason number one: I have a career to think about. I've got my work cut out for me if I plan to make it big as a designer. I couldn't give any man the time he would expect—would even deserve.''

"But I'm such a reasonable man. What are your work hours? Nine-to-five?''

Deni nodded.

"Weekend work?''

Deni shook her head.

"Then there's no problem. You get your days, I get your nights and weekends. Now what's reason number two?''

Addled by that logic, Deni couldn't even think of a good argument. Several moments passed before she offered. "You have a ranch to run. I wouldn't want to take you from your work.''

"Don't worry about that. I'll manage. Now give me reason number three.''

Deni took another deep breath. It seemed all her options were exhausted. Time for the truth. Nothing less than brutal honesty was going to get rid of him.

"You're a cowboy.''

"So we're back to that. What do you have against cowboys, Deni Hadley? What could a woman like you possibly have against a poor ol' cowpoke like me?'' He smiled at her—that smile that took her breath away every time—and leaned back in his chair to await her answer.

"My ex-husband was a cowboy,'' Deni told him coldly. "A good-looking, easygoing, butter-wouldn't-melt-in-his-mouth cowpuncher like you. He took my self-esteem, my trust and my innocence, and stomped them into tiny pieces with those damned two-hundred-dollar boots of his. I'm no fool, Hunter Nash. I learned my lesson. It will be a cold day in hell before I ever love another cowboy.''

Chapter Three

Clearly undaunted, Hunter pursed his lips in a low whistle of respect. "Good reason," he commented solemnly. "How long were you married to your cowboy?"

Deni plopped down in her chair and took a long sip of coffee in a display of nonchalance she didn't feel. Not for the first time she wondered how that ill-fated marriage could still upset her. "Seven lo-o-ng months. And I should be kicked for letting him run my life that long."

"Hell, he's *still* running your life!"

"What are you talking about?" Deni demanded. "I haven't seen Keith Montgomery in ages. He has no hold on me."

Hunter looked at her speculatively through narrowed eyes. "Deni, that man has colored your whole perspective. Not only do you have an irrational prejudice against cowboys, I'll bet you think marriage is for the birds, too."

"As a matter of fact, I do," Deni admitted. "But that's not totally my ex's fault. I have eyes. I know what the divorce rate is."

"Uh-huh. Just what I figured. He's ruined you," Hunter said with a firm nod. "How long have you been divorced, anyway?"

"Eight years," Deni replied somewhat defensively.

"Eight years?" Hunter shook his head in disbelief. "Are you going to let him shadow your life forever?"

"He is *not* shadowing my life!"

"Yes, he is. You're hiding behind the ex even though you know very well that all cowboys aren't deadbeats. I'm willing to bet that at some point in your life you've known at least one worth saving."

Deni sighed, thinking of her brother and of Seth, both certainly cowboys and certainly worth saving. "Maybe one or two," she admitted reluctantly.

"Give me a chance to prove there's another. Let me hang around awhile. Let's see what happens between us. I'm not looking for lifetime commitment here, just a little companionship. So what if we occasionally share a few kisses? That's only natural and we'll just be having the fun two hardworking people deserve." Hunter's eyes were solemn, searching Deni's face.

"No," she replied, her bottom lip jutting out stubbornly. In spite of her short reply, however, she felt more than half tempted to take him up on his offer. She could use a little fun, and cowboy or not, he was so very different from her bum of a husband. Even a fool could see that.

"Come on," he urged, sliding his chair back and getting to his feet. He dropped to one knee beside her.

Of their own volition, her gaze sought his mouth. Unbidden, memories of their kiss washed over her, causing a fluttery feeling in her stomach. As though reading her thoughts, he leaned forward, lightly brushing her parted lips with his. "I dare you to put the past behind you, Denise Hadley," he murmured when he pulled away. "Are you woman enough to risk a relationship with a wrangler?"

Was she woman enough? she wondered, gnawing her bottom lip. In light of the distressing possibility that she had unwittingly let Keith control her outlook on life, Deni decided that she definitely was. Besides, what did she have to lose but a few hours' diversion? She'd been working awfully hard lately what with Christmas just around the corner and the strain of creating her own clothing designs. Didn't she deserve a little entertainment? If things got unpleasant or too hot and heavy, she would simply say her goodbyes and scram.

"I like you. You like me. Let's go for it," Hunter urged, undoubtedly aware of her prevarication.

"All right," she heard herself say. "Let's."

"Hot damn!" He scrambled to his feet, rubbing his palms together gleefully as he paced the room. "We'll start our... uh, association with a trip to Dallas to get your car. Then tonight we'll have that dinner together. I know this really fantastic restaurant you're going to love. I'll call this morning and make a reservation."

She laughed at his excitement, feeling a little of it herself. "What do I wear to this 'fantastic' restaurant?"

"That dress you had on last night looked gorgeous to me," Hunter told her, adding, "did you design it?"

Deni smiled at him, strangely pleased by the compliment. "As a matter of fact I did. But I probably won't wear it again since it was on the pavement for a while. I have others that should do, though.''

"I'll bet your closet would rival Princess Di's,''he teased.

"Actually I don't buy all that many things for myself,'' Deni replied thinking of her cleanly styled business suits and the few dresses she'd managed to have made up from her own designs. "Do you mind if we take my car to the restaurant?''

"You got something against pickup trucks?'' he asked, clearly affronted.

"No, of course not,'' Deni hastily assured him. "Your truck is fine—if you'll get rid of that nasty tobacco.''

Hunter hooted with laughter. "Can't do that. We'll take your car tonight.'' He glanced at his watch. "It's after eight. Are you ready to go get it now?''

"Yes,'' she told him, getting to her feet, too. "Let me get my purse.''

Seconds later, purse in hand, she joined him at the door. He put his hand on the knob as though to open it, but then turned abruptly, catching her up in a bear hug. "You won't regret this,'' he promised solemnly, a seductive gleam in his dark eyes that belied his words. Then he kissed her soundly and opened the door, taking a step back so that she could precede him outside.

Oh, Lordy, Deni thought, easing past him to walk outside. She put her fingertips to her tingling lips. *What have I done?* she asked herself. Did this cowboy have more than friendship on his mind, after all?

Once inside the truck, Deni sat in silence, thinking long and hard about the man getting in next to her. Several adjectives came into her head when she thought of him, and *friend* was certainly not one of them. Instead words like soul mate and, God forbid, lover cropped up.

Am I insane? What has happened to all those promises I made to myself? she wondered gloomily. She thought for a moment of the small farm where she'd spent her formative years and of the parents who still toiled in the fields from sunrise to sunset. They'd never understood their rebellious second child or her frantic need to leave home and move to the city. She, in turn, had never understood their contentment with rural Arkansas life. Did they love being called "rednecks" and having their finances depend on the whim of nature?

Her brother, Stu, had inherited their parents' bent for growing things. Why, he and his wife were in hock to their eyebrows, buying this and that piece of farming equipment. Why had Deni been different? What had made her long for the bright lights, for fame?

And knowing how important her dreams were, why would Deni let a man like Hunter—one who undoubtedly loved the very things she wanted to escape from—into her life on any level?

"Do you mind if we make a little side trip?" Hunter asked, breaking the silence. He put his hand to his hat, adjusting it slightly before he reached to start the engine. It took several tries, and Hunter looked downright relieved when it finally roared to life.

"Where to?" Deni asked suspiciously, hiding a smile.

"My ranch."

"Where, exactly, is this 'ranch' of yours?"

"Mesquite."

"Ahhh, Mesquite. Rodeo country."

"That's right. I guess a woman like you doesn't get to the rodeo much."

"Not much," Deni replied, silently adding, *anymore*. She thought of her barrel-racing trophies safely hidden away in a box in her parents' closet. She thought of the days when she'd been so caught up in the thrills of the local high-school rodeo—pre-Keith days, that is. Happy days.

She'd met her ex-husband at just such a rodeo. What a looker he was: a tall, blond heartbreaker. She would never think of rodeos without thinking of sorrow and she would never go to another one in her life.

"Maybe I'll take you some time. I guarantee you'll love it."

"No!" At her vehement reply, Hunter flicked her a curious glance.

"Don't tell me you're prejudiced against rodeos, too."

"I hate them."

"That's too bad. I love them myself."

Deni flashed him a look of alarm. "Surely you're too old to compete in a rodeo."

Hunter bristled. Just how old did she think he was? "Thirty-two is hardly over the hill."

She frowned. "Are you telling me you do compete?"

Hunter shrugged. "On occasion. The rodeo has been good to me. I made some big bucks a few years back when I competed on a regular basis."

"Bronc rider?"

"That and the bulls. I also tried my hand at a little of everything else, too."

The thought of Hunter astride a bull with fire in its eyes and murder in its heart actually made Deni nauseous. She swallowed hard, saying nothing else, dismayed by her concern for this man she barely knew.

Hunter slid her a sidelong glance, pleased by the alarm written all over her face. Not only had she agreed to go out with this cowboy, but she was blatantly anxious for his welfare. He liked that. It told him he wasn't making a mistake in taking her to his ranch and that his decision to reveal his identity was the right one.

Tactfully Hunter changed the subject to Deni's dress shop and she relaxed visibly. She told him the shop was called Eclat and that she'd been the manager for a couple of years before buying the business from the owner, who was retiring. Her blue eyes flashed, her hands flew about as she animatedly described the changes she'd made so far. Hunter suppressed a sudden, intense desire to pull the truck off the freeway so that he could take her in his arms and kiss her again.

That realization sobered him. She'd agreed to a friendship—nothing more. Friendship was all he wanted. Wasn't it?

After several minutes of thoughtful silence, he spoke again. "We're almost there. Over this next rise on your right."

When they topped the rise, Deni obediently looked to her right, spotting a white frame house sitting away from the road. It was a pretty house—one she wouldn't mind living in herself—with dormant flower beds, big oak trees and a porch swing. *Not bad,* she thought, pleasantly surprised.

Hunter didn't stop there, but went speeding by, commenting, "The next one's mine," Deni automatically looked to where he pointed—looked and nearly died.

"Oh, my God," she breathed, the shock of discovery hitting her full force. Her wide eyes swept the rolling lawn, the tall trees, the enormous split-level home that was a mansion by anyone's standards. *This is a joke,* she assured herself. But one glance at Hunter's proud face told her it was no joke at all. He pulled into the driveway and halted the vehicle.

"Well, what do you think?" he asked, shutting off the engine and opening the door to step out of the truck. He reached inside, pulling her out after him.

Deni was speechless. It seemed she'd been all wrong about Hunter Nash. Mortified, she scanned the rock and roughly hewn cedar dwelling, which seemed to blend with the beauty of the surrounding acres. It was breathtaking—magnificent.

Her mouth was stone dry—her palms damp. Did Hunter have any idea what she'd assumed about his ranch? she wondered thinking back on every conversation they'd had. She couldn't be sure she hadn't revealed her assumptions and the very thought made her face burn with embarrassment. Hesitantly she looked his way and knew immediately that he did, indeed, have a pretty good idea. She could have died.

"It's . . . quite . . . large, isn't it?" she stammered.

"Yep, and not at all what you expected, right?"

Deni gulped and fanned her flaming face with her hand. "Right."

Hunter reached out, cupping her chin in his fingers, raising it so that her eyes locked with his. "I think maybe you let your prejudices get the best of you," he commented softly.

"I think maybe I did," she agreed reluctantly. "I don't quite know what to say."

"No need to say anything," he told her, taking her hand and leading her to the front door. "We all jump to conclusions now and then. Consider this the first of many successful challenges to your crazy notions about

cowboys. Now come on inside. I have something I want
to show you.''

She followed him, managing only a fleeting glimpse
of the long porch, numerous windows and an enormous double door before she was hustled inside. He
immediately led her to the den.

''It's a little messy in here. My aunt cleans for me
once a week on Mondays, so by Saturday the place is a
wreck.'' He strode quickly across the spacious room to
an almost hidden door in one corner.

Dazed, Deni followed more slowly. Her gaze took in
the polished paneling, the rock fireplace, the plush carpet. She noted with an appreciative eye the musket
hanging over the fireplace and the rolltop desk, as well
as the other antiques scattered all around the room.

Very nice, she thought, wishing she could stop and
examine each and every one. But Hunter had said he
had something to show her, and there would be time to
check out the antiques later on in this friendship they'd
agreed upon. Thank goodness they'd come to that understanding *before* she saw his house. After spouting
her opinions of cowboys, she would appear positively
mercenary if she agreed to any sort of relationship now.

''Hurry!'' Hunter urged impatiently, beckoning to
her. ''We've got to go downstairs. You're not going to
believe what I have to show you, but you're going to
love it.''

Curious, Deni followed. She entered the basement
and took a look around, noting they stood in a seemingly normal looking office. What was so special about
that? she wondered. Then her gaze fell on a large,
framed watercolor of a woman in a beautiful dress with
a slight western flair. Deni started in surprise, immedi-

ately recognizing the logo scrawled across the bottom in bold, inch-high lettering: Heart Rustler.

Bewildered, she whirled to face Hunter, who stood watching her reaction in silence, a smug smile on his face. She walked over to the picture to examine it and caught her breath when she read the words scrawled in ink in one corner: To the "boss" with thanks for believing in me when no one else would—Chuck.

Suddenly Deni knew the truth. "You're the mystery man behind Heart Rustler," she stated numbly.

"Yep," he told her with a triumphant grin.

Deni glanced back at the painting, unable to fathom the implications of this revelation. Hunter Nash—savior, cowboy, new "friend"—was also the man she'd risked her neck to meet. It was almost too much to assimilate at once.

The prideful, expectant look on his face told her he knew very well what he could mean to her career. Why on earth hadn't he confessed his true identity when she'd told him barely an hour earlier that she was a designer? That must have been when he figured it out. Or was it?

"How long have you known it was you I was trying to meet last night?"

Hunter's cheeks stained a vivid red. "Uh, a while."

"Be more specific."

He swallowed hard and put the tips of his fingers into his jeans pockets, rocking slightly back on his heels. "I pretty much had it figured out from the beginning."

Deni's chest felt as if it might burst. She drew a shaky breath. "You mean you knew then and you didn't say anything?"

"At first I thought you were a reporter," he told her.

"Oh, for—" she exploded, throwing up her hands in exasperation. "That's the most ridiculous thing I ever heard."

"Not so ridiculous," he argued passionately. "Ever since Heart Rustler hit it big with that advertising campaign on the wall over there, my office manager has been plagued by people trying to meet me—reporters, buyers, department store managers, even the competition, trying to buy me out.... Never mind that I have a designer more than willing to talk about his work, or that I'm not interested in selling out." He shrugged, shaking his head in wonder.

"I can't afford to be in the limelight, you know. That would destroy my credibility as a cattleman. This whole business was just my way of helping out an old college buddy who was down on his luck. Neither of us imagined this kind of fame and glory. I just want to live here in peace with my cattle. That's all. When I realized who Grogan was, I naturally figured you were one of the usual types who haunt the office. I didn't find out differently until after I got home and called Seth."

"All right," Deni said. "I'll buy that, I guess. But why didn't you tell me the truth first thing this morning?"

Hunter hesitated before replying, clearly ill at ease. "I, uh, well, I—"

"Why?" she repeated sternly, though she was now certain she knew the answer.

"All right, I'll tell you. By this morning I'd decided I wanted to get to know you better. I wanted you to agree to go out with Hunter Nash, the cowboy, before I told you everything."

"In other words, you thought I might go out with you so I could use you."

Hunter blanched. "Don't be silly. I just wanted to help you get over your stupid prejudice against cowboys. That's all."

"How very generous of you to donate your precious time to rebuilding my character," Deni said with cold sarcasm. Her throat constricted with barely repressed anger that was building to boiling point. "I can't tell you how much I appreciate the gesture. Why, before I met you I was such a shallow person, using people to get ahead. Now I'm way past all that. I admire you for the honest, trusting cowboy that you really are."

Hunter winced at her bitter words. "Now, Deni—"

"Now, Deni nothing," she retorted. He took a step toward her, as though to catch her arm, but she took a matching step back. "Take me to my car. Now."

"No, not now. When we get a few things straight," he argued, jumping nervously when the phone began to ring.

"I have nothing more to say to you." She began to edge toward the stairs.

"Then just listen," he said, blocking her way and glancing irritably toward the noisy telephone, a very unwelcome intrusion at the moment.

Seeing a chance for escape, she asked. "Aren't you going to get that?"

"No."

"But it might be an emergency."

He started as if just remembering something and lunged for the phone, snatching up the instrument. "Hello?" Deni reached the stairs in four strides, and was all the way to the top of them when she heard him say, "Roy! Where the hell are you?"

She didn't wait to hear anything more, instead making a mad dash across the den, down the short hall and out the front door. She raced to the truck, her heart sinking when she realized the keys were not in the ignition. Now what? she wondered in panic, glancing over her shoulder at the front door. No Hunter yet.

Deni realized she'd left her purse inside the house but wasn't about to go after it even if without it she had no taxi money. She would have to call Seth or maybe Christy, the young woman who helped out in the shop sometimes, she quickly decided, looking hopefully toward the road. But how? She suspected this was a private road; she could see only one other house on it. Without hesitation, Deni started across the lawn at a run, thankful that she was wearing jogging shoes.

Breathless when she reached the neighboring house several yards away, she darted around to the backyard, seeking a door that wasn't in plain view of Hunter's, and then leaned heavily against it, gasping. She looked around the yard, noting the birdbath, the Martin house and the barn. They were familiar sights, and peaceful, too, under other circumstances—but not now. Deni reached up, knocking loudly.

But no one came to the door. After several minutes, Deni admitted defeat, blinking back tears that suddenly filled her eyes *and* threatened to fall. Why hadn't Hunter been honest with her? Were *all* cowboys deceivers like Keith?

Shoulders slumped in dejection, Deni turned to leave. Obviously she was going to have to try to find another phone. At that moment, the door opened. Deni whirled around, her heart leaping with relief. "Oh, thank God," she murmured.

The silver-haired woman at the door took one glance at Deni's flushed cheeks, her wild eyes and her tangled hair, opened the screen door, and asked, "What's wrong?"

"I need some help," Deni told her, absently noting the soft pastel housecoat she wore. "May I borrow your phone?"

The woman glanced over Deni's shoulder, probably looking for an assailant. She hesitated fractionally and then stepped back, letting Deni inside her kitchen. "Do you need to call the police?"

"Oh, no," Deni responded before she thought. Then she frowned. "I mean I don't think so. I don't really know Hunter all that well, but he doesn't seem like the violent type to me. I actually just need to borrow your phone so I can call my cousin to come pick me up. I don't have my car."

Wide green eyes assessed Deni from her tousled hair to her dusty shoes. "Hunter Nash? My neighbor?" Deni nodded. "Why he wouldn't hurt a fly."

"I hope you're right. Now may I borrow your phone?"

The woman, who looked to be anywhere from sixty-five to seventy years old, nodded, pointing to a beige phone hanging on the wall by the refrigerator. Deni hurried over to it, saying a silent prayer that Seth would be home.

Hurriedly she dialed his number. Impatiently she waited to hear his voice, but there was no answer. Deni let it ring and ring before she gave up. She turned to face the woman, who watched her with obvious curiosity.

"No one home?" her hostess asked softly.

"No," Deni responded in dejection. "You don't see Hunter coming, do you? He's bound to figure out where I've gone."

The woman walked to the door, peeking out through the screen. "I don't see anyone." She turned back to Deni, a kind smile on her face. "Why don't you just sit down for a minute, have a drink of something cool, and tell me all about it? You're safe with me, you know. I can handle Hunter with one hand tied behind my back if I have to."

Deni stiffened at the joking comment. Clearly this woman knew her neighbor very well, was probably a good friend of his. Suddenly Deni wanted to leave, wondering if she'd jumped out of the proverbial frying pan into the fire. Her eyes locked with those of the woman who smiled reassuringly and then reached into one of the polished oak cabinets to pull out a glass.

"Iced tea all right?" she asked Deni.

"No, thank you," Deni replied, edging toward the door. "I can't stay."

"Nonsense. How will you get home? You can't go walking up the highway, and besides, he'll see you if you try that. If he comes down here, I'll send him packing." Deni hesitated, wondering if she could trust this stranger. "I promise," the friendly woman added.

Certain she had no other option, Deni reluctantly decided to trust her—at least for the moment. "All right. Seth should be home soon. Then I'll be out of your hair."

"Oh, I'm glad of the company. Now is tea all right?"

"Tea is fine." Deni took one last look out the back door and then walked over to the kitchen table and the chair that had been pulled out for her moments ago. She sat down on the edge of it, ready to take flight if it came to that.

"You sure do smell nice," the older woman said as she handed Deni a frosty glass. "Jasmine, isn't it?"

Deni nodded and took a long sip of the cold amber liquid. Then she took another. Surprisingly she felt somewhat better, and flashed a smile at her companion, who now sat opposite her at the table, her bright eyes checking her out from head to toe. "I don't know how to thank you."

"Don't thank me. I'm pleased to do it. By the way, I don't believe I caught your name."

Deni leaned back in the chair, feeling better by the minute. "Denise Hadley."

A wide smile lighted the face of her hostess. "I'm so pleased to meet you, Denise. My name is Hattie Nash. I'm Hunter's aunt."

Deni gulped, silently bemoaning her faux pas. Of all the people in the world to run to for help, she would have to pick a relative.

"I'm so sorry.... I didn't know...." Deni took a deep breath and tried again. "Please forgive me. I'll leave right now." She set down the glass of tea, getting to her feet immediately.

Hattie's hand reached out to halt her escape. "There's no need for that. I'm an ally." Oddly enough, Deni believed her. Slowly she sat back down, her wide blue eyes never leaving Hattie's green ones. "There. That's better. Now tell me what happened."

"We had an argument," Deni said reluctantly.

"I figured as much. Must have been a humdinger, too, judging from the look on your face when you knocked on my door. Your eyes were as big as cupcakes. I thought the devil himself was after you."

"Hmm," Deni murmured. "That's not a bad description."

Hattie laughed. "Now I'm hooked. Tell me everything."

Deni complied, haltingly and with some emotion. When she'd finished, Hattie shook her head, clucking her tongue. "I don't understand why that nephew of mine is so reluctant to tell the world what he does on the side. No one would think him any less a man, not even those cattlemen friends of his. In fact, if the truth were known, most of them would probably envy his courage in taking such a gamble for a friend."

"What do you mean?"

Hattie sipped her own glass of tea before replying. "I shouldn't be telling you things he hasn't seen fit to tell you himself, but I think you deserve to know the facts. Hunter has an accounting degree from the University of Texas. When he graduated, he worked for two years with a Dallas firm. He made a lot of money, but he hated every minute of it. He's such an outdoorsman— missed the sunshine, the fresh air."

"I can imagine," Deni murmured, thinking of Hunter's deep tan and well-toned body.

"When my husband, Cole, began to have heart trouble about three years ago Hunter jumped at the chance to give up that fancy job to come live with us. He was twenty-nine then and knew Cole would be retiring soon. He intended to buy the place so he took over most of Cole's ranching responsibilities to learn his way around." She glanced at Deni's glass. "Would you like some more tea?"

Deni was surprised to find she had drunk every drop of the refreshing beverage. "Yes, thanks," she replied, adding. "But keep your seat. I don't mind getting it." She walked over to the kitchen door to glance out once more. There was no sign of Hunter. And though relieved, she couldn't help but wonder if his phone call was the reason he hadn't pursued her.

"I have some homemade oatmeal cookies in the jar," Hattie said. "Want one?"

Deni shook her head, hiding her smile. Hattie reminded her of her mother, and for just a moment, Deni missed the parent she hadn't seen in years. Impatiently she pushed those thoughts aside, sitting down and turning her attention back to Hattie. "No thanks. How did a rancher like Hunter get involved in dress design?"

"An old college friend of his, Chuck Masterson, was having some problems and needed help. Chuck was a brilliant designer—still is, in fact—but at that time he couldn't hold down a job because of a drinking problem. He came to Hunter asking for a loan to start his own dress design company. Hunter promised to back him if he'd get some help with his drinking problem. To everyone's surprise, Chuck took him up on his offer and the rest is history, I guess."

"Heart Rustler?" Deni asked softly.

"Yes. Susan Masterson, Chuck's wife, is the office manager, and pretty well runs the business side of things for Hunter, who keeps a low profile. Chuck supervises the Art Department and still manages to find time to draw some himself. The three of them work well together and Hunter's very pleased with their success in spite of the threat to his precious privacy." Hattie reached out and patted Deni's hand. "Surely you can see why he might be loathe to tell you the truth at first."

"Yeah, I guess I can," Deni reluctantly agreed, knowing full well that she, of all people, could hardly blame Hunter for having secrets. Didn't she have a few of her own?

"And you'll forgive him?" Hattie persisted.

"I'll think about it," Deni promised, getting to her feet once more. "Mind if I use your phone again?"

"Go ahead." Hattie got to her feet, too, walking over to the sink to set her glass inside it. Deni saw her glance out the window and noted that the woman tensed.

"Is he coming?" Deni demanded.

"Yes, and on the run."

Deni abandoned the phone and hurriedly joined Hattie at the window, hanging back slightly so she wouldn't be seen from the outside. Hunter was loping across the yard. She could see his agitation, even though he was still some distance away. "I've got to get out of here. I'm not up to another showdown this afternoon. May I use the front door?"

"I have a better idea. You just go hide in the bedroom until I get rid of him. Then we'll figure out how to get you back home."

Deni appraised the woman, wondering again if she could trust a relative of this irate cowboy. Hattie's warm smile convinced her she could. "All right. Thanks."

Hattie pointed to a door. "You can hide in the hall, but watch out for the vacuum cleaner. That's what I was doing when you knocked a minute ago."

Without hesitation, Deni ducked through the door, sidestepping the vacuum cleaner and stopping just inside the hallway so she could hear what was said.

"Did Deni come down here?" Hunter's deep voice boomed a heartbeat after she heard the kitchen door open.

"Who?"

"Denise Hadley, a, uh, friend of mine."

"Have you introduced her to me?" Hattie asked calmly.

Deni almost laughed, imagining Hunter's frustration in the face of his aunt's evasive counterquestions.

"You know I haven't."

"Then how do you expect me to know if she's been here?"

Hunter snorted with impatience. "She's about five-two or three, brownish-blond hair, nice build—"

"Big, blue eyes?" Hattie interjected. Deni could have sworn she heard laughter in the woman's voice.

"She *did* come down here!" Hunter exploded, not at all amused. Deni heard the thud of his boots on the linoleum floor as he strode into the kitchen, and she cringed. What if Hattie gave her away? But Hattie didn't.

"Yes, to use the phone," the woman replied carefully. "You just missed her."

"Damn!" he raged. Deni heard him cross the floor again, heard the door opening.

"Wait, Hunter. You can't leave until you tell me *your* side of what happened," Hattie exclaimed, adding, "And I think you'd better cool down just a little before you go tearing off after Deni anyway."

"I guess you're right," he responded. Deni heard the scrape of a chair being pulled away from the table. "God, what a mess I'm in. If I'd had any idea she'd get so *mad* when she found out about Heart Rustler, I'd have told her first thing this morning."

"You would've?"

"Of course I wou—" he broke off and a long silence followed. Then he admitted, "Well, maybe not."

"Why?" Hattie demanded.

"You know why."

"I have a pretty good idea," his aunt told him. "But I'd like to hear it from you."

"Oh, all right," he grumbled. "I wanted to be sure it was me she was interested in and not a job at Heart Rustler."

"For shame, Hunter Nash! Do you mean to tell me you thought enough of this young woman to drive over to her house at the crack of dawn to take her to her car, and you still believe she would use you?"

There was another long silence and then Hunter exclaimed, "Dammit, Hattie, what's the matter with me? Why can't I ever just go with my gut instinct? Why can't I just trust someone, no questions asked?"

Deni heard the misery in his voice and her heart went out to him in spite of her anger. She could sympathize with his inability to put his faith in anyone. She had that problem herself. As for his deception, she was certainly in no position to pass judgment since she'd been less than honest, too. Maybe if they confronted each other—talked out this misunderstanding—they could begin again.

Begin again? Was that what she really wanted to do? *Yes,* she suddenly realized. She couldn't bear the thought of this cowboy exiting her life as abruptly as he had entered it.

"You and I both know why," Hattie said, adding, "and I'm here to tell you if you don't put the past behind you, you're going to die a lonely old man."

The past? Thoroughly intrigued, Deni abandoned her half-formulated decision to go into the kitchen to confront Hunter. Sure, they needed to talk, but maybe if she waited another couple of minutes she would gain a little insight into his complex character.

"I guess an apology is in order, huh?" Hunter asked his aunt much to Deni's disappointment, though she wasn't really surprised he'd changed the subject. She could tell he was touchy about it.

"Definitely. And the sooner the better," she heard Hattie reply.

"I agree, but it may have to wait until tomorrow. I'm leaving for Tyler in a few minutes."

"Has something happened?"

"Roy just called. Apparently he's married some floozy in Tennessee and won't be back for a couple of weeks. I can't let Lacy stay by herself that long."

Lacy? Deni tilted her head slightly, straining to hear more even as a feeling suspiciously similar to jealousy unexpectedly stabbed her.

"So you're going to get her today?"

"That's right." Deni heard his determination.

"How do you think she's going to feel about big brother storming in and taking over?" Hattie asked.

"I don't give a damn how she feels," Hunter replied. Deni unconsciously released her pent-up breath. So Lacy was his little sister and, from the sound of things, in some kind of trouble. "I'll need to borrow Cole's truck. I've been having a devil of a time getting that one of mine started. All I need is to get stuck down there with an irate teenager on my hands."

"Oh, dear. Cole drove the truck to the sale barn. He won't be back for hours."

Hunter groaned dramatically. "Roy's gone off the deep end, Deni's mad as a hornet and Lacy soon will be *and* Cole's got the truck. What else could possibly happen?"

"We could call a truce long enough for me to drive you to Tyler," Deni ventured softly, stepping into the kitchen, impulsively going with her *own* gut instinct.

Chapter Four

Hunter whirled around at the sound of her voice, exclaiming, "Deni!" before he turned to glare accusingly at his aunt. "You said she was gone."

"I said you just missed her," Hattie corrected him.

"I guess you heard everything," Hunter said to Deni, crossing the room to stand next to her, frowning worriedly.

"Yes," Deni replied. "And I think we need to talk."

Relieved, Hunter drew a deep breath and smiled. "So do I. Were you serious about loaning your car?"

"I never said I'd loan my car," Deni quickly informed him. "I said I'd drive you to Tyler. No one drives my car but me."

When Hattie chuckled, Hunter quickly explained, "It's new," before he turned back to Deni. "Then I accept your offer. We can talk in the car. I *do* think it only fair to warn you that I intend to fetch my half sister, Lacy Beecher, who is seventeen going on thirty, and will *not* want to come home with me. There's bound to be a loud, unpleasant fight."

"If Lacy doesn't want to leave Tyler, then why are you making her?" Deni had to ask, her curiosity getting the better of her.

Hunter shook his head, a look of disgust on his handsome face. "Because my no-account stepfather just called and said he'd eloped with some woman, that's why. He doesn't know when he's coming back and he didn't say a word to Lacy, just ran off and got married. Now it's up to me to tell her she's about to get booted out the door."

"You don't know that for sure," Hattie protested. "Roy loves Lacy. He'll certainly want her to come home when he gets back from his honeymoon."

"And if he does, I'm not going to let her go," Hunter stated flatly. "She wouldn't be welcome. She could never be happy with a stepmother."

"Lacy would be happy anywhere if her dad was around, and you know it. Besides, you have no right to tell her what she can or cannot do."

"I am sick to death of you telling me I have no say in Lacy's life," Hunter roared, his face flushing. "I'm her brother and I love her." He looked at Deni, his features stony. "Do you still want to go?"

"More than ever," Deni replied candidly. At that, Hunter took her hand, pulling her after him as he charged out the door.

Less than an hour later they were in Dallas, getting into her car in the parking lot where she'd left it the night before. Hunter, clearly in control of his temper again, teased, "Sure you don't want me to drive? Think of what this will do to my macho image."

Deni refused to rise to the bait. "I drive."

Shrugging good-naturedly, Hunter got into the car. Deni did the same and in seconds they were headed for Tyler, some hundred miles south.

Once they got clear of the city, Hunter reached out, capturing Deni's hand in his. "Thanks for helping me out," he told her. "You didn't have to, you know."

"I know," she agreed, sassily adding, "And *heaven* knows you don't deserve it. You should have been honest about Heart Rustler Friday night. I wouldn't have nagged you about hiring me."

Hunter winced. "I never thought you would. From what little I've seen of your designs, you'd be an asset, and first thing Monday morning I'm going to get you an interview with Chuck Masterson. He's in charge of the Art Department and always looking for new talent. I'll put in a good word for you. Meanwhile I want you to know I'm really sorry I didn't come clean with you immediately. You've never been anything but honest with me and deserved better."

It was Deni's turn to wince. "Uh, actually, I *have* been less than honest with you and I want to set the record straight right now." She took her gaze off the road long enough to glance at him, noting his dark eyes had widened in surprise. "I'm not from Houston, Texas, at all. I'm from Houston, Arkansas. I grew up on a farm complete with cows, pigs and goats."

Hunter's jaw dropped. Then he hooted with laughter. "I didn't even *know* there was a Houston in Arkansas." He shook his head, smiling broadly. "A farm, huh? Now why would you feel the need to keep a thing like that secret?"

"Being from rural Arkansas has subjected me to a lot of teasing in the past. Some of it was downright cruel, and though I'm not ashamed of my background, it saves a lot of heartache if I just keep it to myself sometimes."

"Well, you sure fooled me and I guess that just goes to show I'm not above jumping to a few wrong conclusions myself."

"Pax?" Deni asked softly.

Hunter leaned toward her, lightly kissing her cheek. "Pax."

"Tell me about your sister, cowboy," Deni said, abruptly changing the subject to hide her threatening emotion.

He grinned at her ruse, but complied. "My sister, or really half sister—we shared a mother—was the kind of baby people snatch from shopping carts: a blond-haired, blue-eyed china doll. I used to live in fear when my stepfather took her somewhere with him. I thought he might forget to bring her back." He laughed shortly. "I know that sounds foolish, but you don't know Roy."

Gently Deni asked, "Your mother's dead?"

Hunter nodded. "Lacy got all Mom's good looks. I worry about her staying alone with Roy since Mom died, not that he would ever lay a hand on her. It's his no-good friends I have qualms about." Hunter shook his head and flashed her a rueful look. "I guess I'm a little overprotective, huh?"

"Maybe, but I don't really blame you." There was a short silence and then Deni exclaimed, "Look! Golden arches. How about some breakfast? We can eat as we go."

"Sounds good to me," Hunter agreed easily. Deni exited the freeway, and pulled into the familiar fast-food chain. It took barely ten minutes to place an order and pay for the food. Then they hit the road again.

Hunter downed his bacon biscuit in two mouthsful and then insisted on feeding Deni her hash brown piece by piece. Obligingly he dipped each morsel in catsup before he handed it to her. She noted that he responded well to her attempts to lighten his mood; he was actually laughing and joking with her, though his tension was still almost tangible.

By the time they reached Tyler and he had directed her to Lacy's driveway, it was a few minutes past ten. She stopped the car and killed the engine. Hunter sat beside her in the car for several minutes, making no move to get out and go to the door. Deni found his nervousness contagious.

"Want me to wait here?" she finally asked uneasily.

He sighed. "Heck if I know." He gave her a heart-rending smile. "Lacy's going to be as mad as all get out; she told me she'd be all right. But dammit, she's only seventeen. If Roy is going to run out on her, she's my responsibility."

Deni reached out, unconsciously massaging the taut muscles at the back of his neck. "Of course she is. You don't have any choice."

"She's a senior this year, you know. She has just a few months of school left. It'll be traumatic if I make her leave Tyler."

"Maybe it won't come to that. Take it a day at a time."

Hunter caught Deni's soothing hand, pulling it around to his lips. He kissed the palm and then tugged her into his arms. "You're good for me, Deni," he said. "I could use a levelheaded woman like you in my life." A heartbeat later, his lips claimed hers.

Levelheaded woman that she was, Deni resisted for a second before she threw caution to the wind and gave in, sliding her hands over his shoulders and behind his head. Her fingers tangled in his thick hair as she opened her mouth, inviting him to deepen the kiss. He complied, thrilling her with his eager response.

His mouth left hers for a moment to nibble her cheek, a caress that left her weak. Framing his rugged jaw with her hands, Deni raised his face back to hers. She needed a breather, but instead of pushing him away, she found herself kissing him again.

"Deni, Deni," he moaned against her skin. "What are you trying to do to me?"

"Make you feel better." Her words were whisper soft against his cheek.

"Holy Moses, honey," he said, releasing her and running his fingers through his tousled hair. "If I get to feeling any better, we're going to get arrested. A man can only stand so much and what you do to me...well, let's just say I'm going to have to cool down considerably before I face my very observant baby sister."

Hunter opened the car door. He looked back before he stepped out, and groaned softly, closing his eyes tight.

"What's wrong?" Deni demanded.

"You look...thoroughly kissed. Better wait a few minutes before you come in, but be sure you *do* come in. I suspect I'm going to need your help to get her to go back with me. Roy hasn't told her about the wedding yet, and I'm not quite ready to break it to her, either. She thinks he'll be home in a few days." With that prediction he left Deni, who was slightly dazed, to stride across the yard to the front door, where he stood for several moments before knocking.

Deni watched him until he finally disappeared into the house. Then she glanced in the rearview mirror, noting her flushed cheeks and bright eyes. What had he said? That she looked thoroughly kissed? Well, not only did she look that way, but she felt that way, too. She realized she might have to give him more than a few minutes with his sister since it would definitely take longer than that to get her pulse rate back to normal and erase the telltale bloom in her cheeks.

What is wrong with me? she agonized for the umpteenth time since she'd met Hunter Nash. What was it about that man that stole her common sense, challenged years of bad feelings toward cowboys, farms, rodeos and the sadness those things inevitably brought? And how could one simple kiss affect her this way?

Deni waited a good ten minutes before she ventured across the yard to the porch. Hesitantly she peeked through the screen door into the cozily furnished living room.

Hunter spotted her at once. He got to his feet and hurried to let her inside, his eyes sweeping over her. His hot-blooded assessment destroyed her freshly won composure. Deni felt her face burning. She found she could not meet his intense gaze.

"Deni," he said rather huskily, pulling her into the room. "This is my sister, Lacy Beecher. Lacy, Deni Hadley, a new friend."

Lacy's pretty oval face was sullen, a fact that didn't surprise Deni. No doubt Hunter had shared his plans to relocate her and she wasn't thrilled by them.

"Nice to meet you," Deni said, smiling warmly. "Hunter has told me a lot about you."

"Too bad I can't say the same," Lacy muttered, eyeing her suspiciously. She turned to Hunter, her clear blue eyes accusing. "I'm not going with you."

"Yes, you are," he retorted calmly. "Now go pack your bag."

"No. Dad might try to call, and besides, I hate that stupid ranch of yours."

"You'll have a room of your own," Hunter entreated. "We'll get you some wheels. Your Aunt Hattie will do the cooking. What more could you want?"

"I want my dad, that's what I want. I just know he'll be home any time. And Hattie's not *my* aunt, she's yours. She and Cole both hate Dad, and I hate them. Besides, I told you last night that I'm not leaving Tyler before school's out."

Seeing Hunter's tensed body and sensing he was about to explode, Deni stepped in, surprising herself and him when she spoke. "Maybe you won't have to stay with Hunter. I have a house in Garland and I have a spare bedroom."

"That's out of the question," Hunter interjected immediately.

"Why?" Lacy demanded as though grabbing this chance to goad him. She cocked her head, unabashedly appraising Deni as a possible ally. Then she smiled, apparently coming to a decision. "I'd like to stay with Deni."

"No way and that's final." Hunter's voice was firm.

"Why?" Lacy demanded again.

"Yes, why?" Deni echoed. "It won't hurt anything if she stays with me a night or two. As soon as you hear something definite from her father, we'll take it from there."

Hunter paced the room as he always did when thinking. Out of the corner of his eye, he saw Deni and Lacy exchange a conspiratorial wink. After a rather shaky beginning, the pair actually seemed to be hitting it off.

As a result he could sense a lessening of the tension between himself and his sister. What a blessing that was, and having her at Deni's house would give him the perfect excuse to visit. Then there was the added boon that once he got his sister away from Tyler, it would be much easier to talk her into moving to his ranch for good.

"All right," he said. "Since Deni was kind enough to ask you, you can stay with her."

Lacy jumped to her feet, catching him in a hard hug. "Thanks, Hunter. I'll pack my bag—just enough for the weekend, of course."

"Of course," he agreed dryly.

While they waited, Deni walked over to the faded couch and sat down. She patted the seat beside her, smiling an invitation. Hunter joined her.

"Tell me something about your mother," she said softly, glancing at a photograph on the doily-draped coffee table. "Is that her?"

Hunter picked up the old eight-by-ten and nodded. "Yeah, that's her. She died of cancer about four years ago. She had a hard life, first with my dad dying when I was ten and then marriage to a—" he glanced toward the hallway and lowered his voice "—good-for-nothing like Roy when I was fourteen."

"I take it you didn't get along with your stepdad."

"We barely tolerated each other from day one. He got laid off from his job off and on. He and Mother fought a lot. Then Lacy came along and he was laid off for good. I became an extra mouth to feed. When I was eighteen, I ran away and moved in with my aunt and uncle in Mesquite."

"Your aunt is such a sweetheart," Deni said, her heart aching for him. "I can't imagine why Lacy doesn't like her."

"I don't think Lacy really meant what she said. Aunt Hattie is my real dad's sister. She and Cole feel as I do about Roy and I guess Lacy has picked up on it." Hunter broke off when Lacy entered the room, an overnight case in her hand.

"Well, let's go if we must," she grumbled. "But I have to be back by Monday. I just know Dad'll be home by then."

"We'll work that out tomorrow," Hunter responded, exchanging a worried look with Deni. He took Lacy's bag and led the way to the door.

While Deni drove back to Garland, Hunter sat in silence in the back seat, listening to the two women chatter. Lacy asked Deni question after question about her personal life and Hunter listened with avid interest as she patiently answered each one. He found out that in college, she had majored in business and minored in art. He also learned a little more about her dress shop than she'd told him before.

He also found out that she loved potatoes—fixed any way—Andrew Wyeth paintings and antiques. Hunter smiled to himself, noting that as Lacy's questions got more and more personal Deni's replies got more and more brief.

Good-naturedly he decided to get her off the hook. "We'll be at Deni's in no time, Lacy. I think you'll like her house. It has a lot of antiques in it."

"Hang around there a lot, do you?" Lacy asked, openly curious about her brother's relationship with Deni.

"Now don't you go jumping to any conclusions about Deni and me," Hunter cautioned sternly. "We just met last night and we're friends, nothing more."

"I see," Lacy replied. "And the lipstick on your collar is Aunt Hattie's?"

Damn. Hunter didn't know how to respond to that. Clearly he was going to have to be more careful if he wanted to set a good example for Lacy.

"That's catsup," Deni interjected smoothly. "We ate on the road a while ago."

"Oh." Lacy's disappointment was evident. "And you really *are* just friends?"

"I'm afraid so," Deni told her.

"Too bad. You two would make a lovely couple. You complement each other."

An uncomfortable silence followed that observation and lasted until Deni pulled her car into the Dallas parking lot where Hunter's truck was parked. He got out of the car and then bent down, peering inside. "Are you sure you'll be all right, Lacy?"

"Of course she'll be all right," Deni told him.

"You've got my number if you need me," he said.

"Yep." Lacy reached up, throwing her arms around his neck, hugging him tightly. "Bye, Hunter."

"Bye."

"My brother's wild about you," Lacy noted with a sly smile forty minutes later. She and Deni were changing the linen on the bed in the spare bedroom at Deni's house.

The older woman glanced uneasily at Lacy, who stood on the other side of the bed, smoothing the pale lavender top sheet. She'd felt the younger woman's heavy stare ever since they'd entered the room. "Excuse me?"

"He thinks you're really hot. What do you think of him?"

Flustered by the direct question, Deni reached for the fluffy comforter, pulling it up over the bed. "I think he's . . . very nice," she hedged, keeping her eye on her task.

"Nice?" Lacy threw up her hands in disgust. "Is that the best you can do? Why, his girlfriend thinks he's sexier than Tom Selleck."

Girlfriend? Deni caught her breath, her eyes locking with Lacy's twinkling ones.

"Gotcha!" Lacy exclaimed with a jubilant laugh. "I just *knew* there was something between you two."

"There really isn't, you know," Deni argued, her cheeks glowing. "I *do* like him, of course, and maybe he likes me. But neither of us is looking for romance." She picked up a pillow, stuffing it into the pillow sham.

"Why ever not? You're both single. Anyone can see you're attracted to each other." Lacy reached for the other pillow and did the same.

"But it takes more than mere attraction to make a relationship," Deni told her. "We have a few things in common, but we have totally different values and goals."

Lacy heaved a sigh and sat on the edge of the freshly made bed. "I understand. I guess I was just hoping." She flashed a smile. "This is going to be much better than the ranch. I sure am glad you asked me to stay with you."

"So am I. Now why don't we make a run to the grocery store? We'll get something special—something we both like. Then maybe we'll call that brother of yours and ask him over for dinner. What do you think about that idea?"

"You've got my vote," Lacy told her, grinning.

* * *

They were inseparable most of the day, getting to know each other while they bought groceries, toured Garland and visited Deni's dress shop. Then they spent the rest of the afternoon rearranging the spare bedroom. To no one's surprise, Hunter accepted the dinner invitation with enthusiasm when Lacy called him.

Midafternoon, the doorbell rang. Thinking it might be Hunter, arriving early to check up on Lacy, Deni hurried to the back door. To her delight, Seth stood on her porch, dressed in tattered sweats and a bright orange muscle shirt.

"Hi, Deni," he said, smiling that old smile she remembered from saner times. She smiled back with difficulty, reaching out to grasp his hand and tug all six-foot-three of him into the kitchen.

"You're in big trouble, kiddo," she told him, shaking a finger under his nose.

He howled with laughter. "Listen, I'd betray my *mother* for Dwight Yoakam tickets."

"I'm going to tell her you said that," Deni warned, but she was laughing too. "Have a seat. I'll get you a cola."

"I can't stay," he told her. His smile faded and he shuffled his feet, suddenly looking a little uneasy. "Actually I came by to ask two questions."

"So ask me," Deni said, amused by her cousin's sudden discomfort.

"Are you going home for Thanksgiving, week after next?"

Deni's amusement vanished. "Who wants to know?"

"I do," Seth replied, but his eyes wouldn't meet hers.

"Actually I probably won't. I have a new roommate and it's a busy time of year for me at the shop."

Seth cleared his throat nervously. "Mom called me this afternoon."

Uh-oh, Deni thought. *Here it comes.* "What'd she have to say?"

"Oh, nothing much," he hedged. "She'd just heard from Aunt Faye."

"And how is my mother?"

"Pretty depressed from what I hear. She wants to see you. She's hoping you'll come home the Wednesday before the holiday and stay until the weekend at least. I promised Mom I'd find out what your plans are."

Deni walked to the counter and busied herself de-boning the chicken she'd stewed earlier. "I guess you'd better tell her I won't be able to make it. Maybe next year things won't be so hectic."

"How long has it been since you went home?" Seth asked softly.

Deni shrugged and kept working, refusing to look at her cousin who was now standing right behind her. "A couple of years, I guess," she lied, knowing full well it had been four.

He grasped her shoulders, turning her to face him. "Do you hate the farm so much?" he asked. His blunt question did not offend Deni. It reminded her of the days before Seth's father moved his medical practice and his family from Arkansas to Texarkana, Texas, during her senior year in high school. Although Seth was several years younger, he and Deni had always visited whenever possible, sharing every secret, perhaps because they recognized the rebel in each other.

"Not really," Deni murmured. "I just don't feel comfortable there."

"Are you embarrassed that your parents are farmers? Is that it?"

Deni bristled at the question. "Seth Hadley! You know me better than that. I love my parents."

"Going home once every ten years is a fine way to show it," Seth noted dryly.

"So all of us aren't as dedicated as you," Deni countered, adding, "and I might go home every other weekend, too, if my folks were like yours." She reached out, ruffling his shaggy hair. "By the way, what do they say about *this*?"

"Mother offers me money for a haircut. Dad asks me if I've found any spiders nesting in it yet."

Although Seth spoke lightly, Deni knew he spoke the truth. Her eyes filled with tears. "No lectures?"

Seth shook his head, visibly chagrined by her display of emotion. He patted her shoulder awkwardly. "You used to get along with your folks. What happened, the divorce?"

"That started it, I guess," Deni said, brushing impatiently at a tear that had snaked its way down her cheek. Seth handed her a bandanna and she dabbed at her eyes, trying not to smear her mascara. "Even though neither of them liked Keith, they both believe marriage means 'till death do us part'—even if it's to a cowboy with a roving eye. Dad figured I got what I deserved for eloping graduation night. He wanted me to marry Stu's friend, George, and spend the rest of my life having babies and cleaning house."

Seth smiled in sympathy. "A fate worse than death?"

Deni drew a shuddering breath and nodded, swiping at the tears that kept coming. "Mom couldn't understand why I wouldn't move back home after the divorce. But I had to prove I could get by on my own."

At that moment Lacy, who'd been watching television in the living room, walked into the kitchen, an empty glass in hand. She stopped short when she saw her new friend's distress and rushed over to Deni, glaring at Seth as though he were responsible.

"What's wrong?" she demanded hotly. "What did he do to you?"

In spite of her tears, Deni almost laughed at Seth's expression—a mixture of outrage at Lacy's assumption as well as obvious appreciation for the teenager's blond good looks. "He didn't do anything. We were just, uh, reminiscing. This is my cousin, Seth Hadley. Seth, this is my roommate, Lacy Beecher."

Seth nodded solemnly. Lacy flicked him a contemptuous look and then dismissed him, turning back to Deni. "Are you okay?"

"Fine." Sensing Lacy's doubt, Deni added, "Really."

After a fractional hesitation, Lacy nodded. She walked over to the sink, deposited her glass there and turned, walking slowly back to the door, her accusing eyes never leaving Seth. Then, without another word, she disappeared into the living room.

"That's your roommate?" Seth whispered when she was out of sight. "She's just a kid. I thought maybe your cowboy had moved in with you, which brings me to my second question. How did he make out with you?"

"Seth!" Deni scolded. Then she chuckled. "Actually this is the cowboy's sister. She's staying with me for a while."

Seth smiled knowingly at that news. "And that means he'll be hanging around, too."

Deni shrugged. "Probably."

Seth laughed. "I thought you and cowboys didn't mix."

"Oddly enough, he's one of the nicest men I've ever met, and cowboy or not, I'd trust him with my life."

"What about your heart?"

She shook her head doubtfully. "My heart's not even in question."

"I hear you," Seth said, with a grin, moving toward the door. "Keep me posted. Meanwhile think about going home again. People *do* change, you know. Things might look different this time around."

Deni didn't reply to that, giving him a wan smile. Halfway across the kitchen, he halted and turned back to her. "Does Lacy date anyone?"

"I don't really know," Deni replied, somehow not surprised by the question. "She hasn't mentioned anyone, but I can't believe she doesn't."

"Me, either. Well, so long."

With that, he walked out the door, giving her a jaunty wave. Deni stood by the table for several minutes after he left, motionless and lost in thought. *Do* people change? she wondered. Had she matured through the years? Her mixed feelings toward Hunter were a pretty good indication she might have mellowed somewhat. And what about her parents? Had they, perhaps, mellowed as well?

She knew they loved her; they'd shown it in a million ways during her childhood and even after her disastrous marriage. But Deni believed that love to be conditional—a smothering love. Her older brother had led a charmed life, making good grades, carrying on in his father's footsteps, marrying well. And then along came Deni; rebellious, blundering through life, hating school and the farm.

Although Deni blamed no one but herself for her hasty marriage to a young cowboy she'd met at the state livestock show, she also knew that she would never have married him if her parents hadn't objected so strongly to the relationship in the first place. For her Keith was a means of escape. He was fun; he was fascinating; he was forbidden. What more could a young girl, who was longing for more than life on a small Arkansas farm, possibly ask?

She'd soon regretted her rash decision to elope, of course, finding that he was also folly. His promises of a bright future were lies. He never worked hard at anything but chasing rodeo queens, a task he took quite seriously and at which he excelled. He tormented Deni relentlessly about her rural roots. It didn't take her long to realize she'd made a mistake, but her considerable pride wouldn't let her go back home. She'd moved to Morrilton, rented a room and worked two jobs until she had saved enough money to move to Texas. There she qualified for a work scholarship at Texas State. She'd studied hard, graduating in three years and a summer, stubbornly refusing any financial help from the parents who always had advice to offer and something to say about what she was doing with her life.

The time between visits got longer and longer until Deni stopped going home altogether. Now more than differences in values separated Deni from her parents. There were differences in life-style, as well, not to mention the physical miles between them—miles she'd vowed never to travel again.

Chapter Five

"What, no potatoes?" Hunter teased Deni a couple of hours later in her kitchen. Lacy sat on his left, Deni across from him at the beautifully set table. He drank in the sight of Deni's blue sweater, which hugged full, feminine curves and exactly matched her sparkling eyes. With difficulty he dragged his own eyes back to her glowing face, not for the first time reminding himself they were friends—nothing more.

"Potatoes with chicken and dumplings?" she asked in disbelief, oblivious of his heated inspection.

Hunter laughed. "I guess that might be a bit much. My compliments to the chef, by the way."

"Thank you," Deni answered, obviously pleased.

"I made the salad," Lacy ventured.

"And the salad's fantastic," Hunter hastily responded, getting a big smile for his efforts. "So how was your first day in Garland, sis? Tell me what you did."

"Well, let's see," Lacy responded, tilting her head as she thought, a move that made her shoulder-length curls fall over her face. Impatiently she tossed them back. "Deni and I went to the grocery store."

"I'll bet that was exciting," Hunter teased, reaching out to tug a strand of her silvery-blond hair.

"A thrill a minute," Lacy agreed, laughing. She slapped his hand away. "Then we went to Deni's shop."

"Yeah?"

"Uh-huh. It's really nice, too. I found a dress I like. Deni said it looked like it was made *for* me."

Hunter groaned. "Thank you, Miss Hadley. Lacy *needs* another dress," he said sarcastically. "What else did you do?"

"We rearranged the bedroom," Lacy told him, "and I watched a movie. I guess that's about all. Oh, yeah, some guy came by to see Deni."

"Seth," Deni explained to Hunter.

"So what did you think of Seth?" Hunter asked his sister.

"I didn't like him. He made Deni cry."

Hunter started in surprise. He leaned slightly forward across the table, frowning at the woman across from him. "Is something wrong at home? Did Seth have bad news?"

"No, no. Nothing like that," Deni assured him, hoping to discourage further questions. She toyed with her food, her appetite suddenly gone. "He was just trying to find out if I'm going home for Thanksgiving."

"And that made you cry?" Hunter persisted.

Deni shrugged away his question. "I don't get along very well with my parents," she said, concentrating on buttering a delicately browned square of corn bread she really didn't want to eat. "I haven't been home in a while, and he was sort of fussing at me."

"Exactly how long has it been since you went home?" Hunter asked sternly.

Immediately on the defensive because of his recriminating tone, Deni hedged, "Oh . . . years."

Hunter's eyes narrowed speculatively. "How many years?"

"Hey!" Lacy suddenly exploded, rising to her new friend's defense. "Maybe it's none of your business, big brother."

"I'm just asking a simple question," he told her. "Deni needs to keep in touch with her parents."

Lacy hooted with laughter. "*That* from *you*?"

Hunter had the grace to look embarrassed. "So I don't want her to make the same mistakes I made. Besides, I would have gone home more often if Roy—" He halted abruptly, glancing quickly at Lacy as if he had second thoughts about what he was going to say.

"Go ahead and say it. You would have come home more often if Dad had made you welcome." She sighed heavily, her face growing sad as she obviously remembered why she was at Deni's. "Where could that dad of mine be? I wish I was in Tyler. I'm sure he's tried to call by now and missed me."

"Just because your dad hasn't gotten in touch with you, doesn't mean he doesn't love you," Deni said, glaring accusingly at Hunter, who squirmed in his chair. He knew just what she was thinking, and she certainly was right. He should have told Lacy the truth by now. But he'd held back, hoping he would hear from Roy so that he would be able to tell her when to expect her father home again.

"I know he loves me," Lacy declared defensively. "It just seems like he could call."

"He'll call," Hunter snapped. He immediately regretted ventilating his frustration, and added in a much softer tone of voice. "Just don't worry, okay?"

Lacy swallowed hard, mumbling, "Okay."

"Anybody want dessert?" Deni asked brightly in an obvious effort to lighten the mood.

"Sure," Hunter told her, belatedly asking, "What is it?"

Lacy managed a smile. "As if it mattered."

"Apple pie," Deni told him. She turned to Lacy. "Would you mind getting the ice cream? It's in the freezer in the laundry room."

"All right." Lacy got to her feet and left the kitchen. Hunter was not surprised when Deni turned on him.

"You'd better tell your sister the truth and quick," she whispered angrily.

"I'll tell her. I'll tell her," Hunter whispered back. "Just as soon as I have something to tell. I've been trying to call Roy all afternoon to let him know where she is. Can't get hold of him."

"I'm giving you until tomorrow, then I'm going to do it for you," Deni warned, breaking off when Lacy walked back into the kitchen, ice cream in hand. Hunter sat in thoughtful silence while the two women readied the pie, half wishing Deni would do it. He was sure she would do a better job.

After they were all stuffed and miserable, they cleared the table and played a game of Uno. To Deni's chagrin, Hunter won every hand of the fast-paced card game, and then gloated about it. With great pleasure she invited him to leave nearly two hours later, claiming it had been a long day and ignoring his knowing smile.

He got to his feet good-naturedly and walked around the table to his little sister. "I'll see you tomorrow," he told her.

"Not too early," she told him. "I'm planning on sleeping late."

Nodding his agreement, Hunter kissed her. Then he automatically turned to do the same to Deni, but stopped when her eyes widened in alarm.

Lacy laughed aloud at his quandary. "Go ahead and kiss your 'friend,'" she said, a smug smile on her face. "I won't look."

"I was just going to thank her for supper," Hunter responded, his face flushing.

"Sure you were," she replied.

Hunter grasped Deni's hand, pulling her to her feet and then out the door away from Lacy's eager eyes. There he took her in his arms. "I don't know how to thank you for helping me out with Lacy."

"No need to thank me," she replied. "I think this is going to be fun. Now you'd better beat it. Lacy's at a very impressionable age. I don't want our attraction to be so obvious."

Hunter laughed. "So now you're admitting you're attracted to me. Fine time to tell me that—when I can't do much about it."

Not surprisingly, he then did what he'd just said he couldn't do—he captured her lips with his.

Deni, however, already rued her thoughtless admission, even though she knew he'd probably suspected how she felt without her telling him. She needed time to get used to the idea of having this cowboy around— knew she had to keep her head on straight and take things slow. Obviously she couldn't do that when he was kissing her. With great difficulty she kept her body rigid and her mind on the young woman in the kitchen, who was, no doubt, dying of curiosity.

As though sensing defeat, Hunter released her. "All right. I get the message. I'll go. But I'm here to warn you I might not always be so easy to get rid of."

"Yeah?" she asked softly, a sweet thrill unexpectedly sending goose bumps dancing over her arms.

"Yeah," he whispered. Deni was certain that the gleam in his eye had nothing whatsoever to do with reflection.

Hours later, she lay in her bed, wide-eyed and wide awake, her thoughts running wildly in all directions—chasing possibilities and rehashing certainties. How did she feel about Hunter Nash? she kept asking herself. Why was she so drawn to him? She'd dated several men in the past few years—desirable men with white-collar jobs, the kind of man she thought she wanted to marry someday. Why hadn't she lost sleep over any of *them*?

What made Hunter so special? Was it his personality that attracted her—that intriguing blend of rake and gentleman? It certainly seemed that each one of Hunter's predictable cowboy traits—the ones her short-lived marriage had taught her to expect—had a surprisingly endearing characteristic to offset it. He'd said he was going to challenge her prejudices. Well, he was doing a fine job of it.

Deni stared through the dark, watching the silhouette of the windowpanes play over the wall and then the ceiling as a car drove by outside. She heard the thud of the Sunday newspaper hitting the driveway. She realized she might as well get up. It looked like she wouldn't get any sleep until she came to some kind of decision about Hunter.

Obviously he liked her. His kisses—and there had already been far too many of them—said as much. She suspected her kisses said the same to him, and that meant they were moving much too fast. She wasn't ready to get involved in more than the friendship they'd agreed upon. Somehow she had to slow things down until she sorted out her feelings. But how?

Deni moaned softly. She closed her eyes and turned over restlessly in bed, hugging her pillow like it was the man who'd kept her awake all night. A soft knock sounded on the door. Deni opened her eyes, unsure she had really heard anything.

"Deni?"

It was Lacy. Clearly Deni wasn't the only one with a troubled mind. "Come in," Deni called, sympathizing with the younger woman's problem.

The door opened just enough for Lacy to stick her head inside. "I'm sorry I woke you up. I—I just can't sleep."

"Neither can I." Deni sat up and tossed back the covers on the other side of the bed. "I haven't turned on the central heating yet, so it's as cold as a Colorado winter in here. Hop in."

Lacy didn't need a second invitation. She scampered across the floor, leaping onto the bed. Deni could hear her teeth chattering as she pulled the blanket and coverlet over her shivering body.

"Bad dream? Or just too much to think about?" Deni asked softly.

"Too much to think about. There's something you and Hunter aren't telling me, isn't there?"

Deni hesitated, not really sure it was her place to tell Lacy the truth about her father in spite of her earlier warning that she intended to do exactly that. "Yes, there is. But I think Hunter needs to tell you himself."

"No, you tell me. I can't bear to hear it from him. He can't help but gloat when Dad does something stupid...." She broke off, crying quietly.

That did it. "Your dad got married again. Hunter was waiting to get some more details before he told you."

"Oh, no." For several moments, all Deni heard were muffled sobs. Finally Lacy seemed to get control of herself. "So Dad's going to be gone for a long time, then?" Her voice was strained. Deni's heart went out to her.

"Maybe. We're not sure."

"That means Hunter won't let me go back home. He thinks I'm a baby, you know." She sniffed loudly.

"How would you manage on your own? Do you have a car? An income?"

"I can manage. I'll get a job, and I have friends who'll take me to school."

"But Lacy, this is your senior year. You're supposed to be having *fun*. Soon you'll be in college, studying hard, possibly working, and these teenage days will be gone forever. If you stay with Hunter, he can help provide for you."

"But I'll have to move—leave all my friends," she protested tearfully.

"A beautiful girl like you won't have any problems making new friends," Deni assured her. "Why every boy in Mesquite will be begging you for a date."

"Think so?"

"Know so."

"But I don't want to live in Mesquite. Hunter's Aunt Hattie and Uncle Cole are there. I can't stand the way they look at me, like it's my fault Hunter ran away from home. Besides, Hunter is too bossy. He doesn't think I have any brains. He'd never let me go anywhere."

Deni could only agree with Lacy on that score since she'd thought of that herself the minute Hunter mentioned getting Lacy to move in with him. He would be overprotective in the extreme, much like her parents had been, and that would mean trouble for everyone. She sat in thoughtful silence for a minute before the first glimmer of an idea brightened her horizon. Maybe she could act as a buffer between this troubled teenager and her brother, share some of her own hard-learned lessons. At the same time, she would gain valuable time— get to know Lacy's brother better. "You could move in with me."

Lacy caught her breath. "You mean you'd let me live here? With you?"

"Why not? I have enough room, and to be perfectly honest, I'd like the chance to get to know both you and Hunter better."

"But do you think we can talk that brother of mine into it?" Lacy asked, clearly excited. She sniffed again.

Deni smiled, pleased by her elation, and handed her a box of tissues from the nightstand. "I don't know, but it's certainly worth a shot. We'll have to work out a strategy—ease into this gradually—make it the most desirable choice."

"Oh, my," Lacy said with a sigh. "I don't know how on earth we're going to manage that."

"You just leave it all to me," Deni told her firmly. "I'm used to dealing with stubborn cowboys." To her surprise, Lacy threw her arms around her neck.

"Thanks, Deni, I'll never forget this."

"You're welcome. Now try to get some sleep. We've got to keep our wits about us today."

"Can I stay in here with you?"

"Sure."

Lacy shifted farther down under the covers and heaved a sigh. She was silent for so long that Deni thought she slept. Then Lacy said, "Deni?"

"Hmm?"

"I'm glad you want to get to know my brother better."

Deni made no reply to that, smiling to herself. Lacy reminded her so much of herself at that age: vulnerable, defensive, insecure. Maybe she could help her through these troubled times. And if she and Lacy's big brother got to be more than friends, that just might be all right, too.

It was nearly noon Sunday when Hunter pulled his uncle's truck into Deni's driveway. He steeled himself for the meeting with his sister, knowing she was not going to like the decision he'd come to after he'd finally reached his stepfather late the night before.

Much to Hunter's surprise, Roy had actually been relieved to hear about Lacy's move. The astounding reason behind the man's unexpected relief had sent Hunter back to Tyler early that morning.

Now he got out of the truck and walked to the back, checking to be sure he'd arrived with his load intact. He perused all Lacy's worldly possessions, hoping he hadn't forgotten anything important. Admittedly his decision to drive to Tyler alone had been an impulsive one, but he hadn't dared take his sister with him. With his luck, she would have locked herself in the bath-

room or used some other dramatic, teenage ploy to foil
his attempts to help her. Now he had leverage. He
would tell her as much of the truth about Roy as he
dared, and make her see that this was the only way to
handle their problem.

Hunter stooped down, picking up the newspaper that
still lay on the driveway. Whistling to boost his courage, he strode toward the kitchen door under the carport. To his surprise it was closed and securely locked.

Something was wrong, he decided immediately. He
glanced at his watch. It was five minutes until noon.
Surely they weren't still sleeping. Curious and a little
worried, Hunter rang the bell. He waited three inter-
minable minutes before ringing it again.

"I'm coming," Deni called from behind the door.
"Hold your horses."

Hunter smiled at that. She must have been in the
shower or something. She was probably wrapped in a
towel, her honey-colored hair soaked and dripping over
that peachy skin of hers....

Was that any way to think about a friend? he asked
himself sternly, swallowing hard. In spite of that re-
minder, his heart began to thud and his body responded to that vivid thought. The door opened. Deni
reached to unlock the screen.

"Sorry," she mumbled, obviously still half asleep. "I
guess I overslept." She pushed open the door.

Hunter stepped inside, careful not to let his tensed
body touch hers. He knew one false move might send
him over the edge of control, and it would never do to
have Lacy see him assaulting her host on the kitchen
table. He couldn't stop his eyes from caressing the
woman before him, however. Her sleep-tousled hair
gave her an incredibly sexy appeal, tempting him to

forget he wanted nothing more than friendship from her. He filed that thought away for future reference, refusing to think about it now.

"I brought in your newspaper," he said, laying it on the table. He glanced toward the hallway. "Lacy still asleep, too?"

Deni nodded and combed her hair back from her face with her fingers. "We both had a bad night, I'm afraid. She was worried about her dad; I was worried about ... well, things."

Secure in the knowledge that Lacy was still in bed, Hunter allowed himself one step toward the woman he found so incredibly appealing. "What things?"

"Never mind," she said, moving to slip past him. He caught her arm, halting her progress and then pulling her back to him. He had to kiss her good morning. That's all there was to it. Just one kiss—one quick kiss—and he would let her go. Hungrily his lips took hers, all his good intentions flying right out the window.

Deni knew she should resist. So why did she stand so docilely, clutching his shirt in case her knees gave way? It seemed all her resolutions of the night before were for naught. She gloried in the taste of him—wanted more.

Luckily he broke off the kiss, raising his head to again ask, "What things?"

She sighed. "You and me things."

"So I'm not the only one wondering about us," he murmured, releasing her. He drew in a fortifying breath and plunged ahead. "Deni. I'm thinking I want to be just a little more than a friend to you. How do you feel about that?"

"Cooperative," she admitted.

Hunter released his breath in a slow whoosh that made Deni smile. "I was hoping you'd say that. We need to talk and now would be a good time."

"Yes, it—"

"Was that my brother?"

Hunter and Deni both jumped at the sound of Lacy's sleepy call. They broke apart instantly.

"It's me all right," Hunter called out in a voice that sounded suspiciously husky even to his own ears. "It's about time you woke up, lazybones."

By the time Lacy entered the kitchen, bleary-eyed and yawning, Deni had collapsed in a chair. The newspaper was spread out before her, opened to the sports page, of all things. Hunter stood by the counter, pouring himself a cup of coffee. He took a sip and nearly choked.

Deni laughed. "I set the timer for eight o'clock. That might be a tad strong by now."

Nodding his agreement, he pulled open a drawer, locating a spoon at once. Then he retrieved the cream from the refrigerator, top shelf, right-hand side. Deni's face burned as she watched Lacy watch her brother reach toward the four identical canisters on the counter, and on first try find the one that held the sugar.

Lacy grinned triumphantly, crossing her arms over the burnt orange football jersey that served as a nightshirt. Although she made no comment, it was clear that she knew Hunter had drunk morning coffee in this kitchen before. Deni sagged in the chair. No doubt they were going to have to field another thousand questions about their feelings toward each other—questions neither of them were ready to answer. What else could possibly go wrong today? she wondered.

"Did you ask him yet?" Lacy blurted out.

NO COST! NO OBLIGATION TO BUY!
NO PURCHASE NECESSARY!

PLAY "LUCKY 7"
AND GET AS MANY AS SIX FREE GIFTS...
HOW TO PLAY:

1. With a coin, carefully scratch off the silver box at the right. This makes you eligible to receive one or more free books, and possibly other gifts, depending on what is revealed beneath the scratch-off area.

2. You'll receive brand-new Silhouette Romance™ novels. When you return this card, we'll send you the books and gifts you qualify for *absolutely free!*

3. Unless you tell us otherwise, every month we'll send you 6 additional novels to read and enjoy. If you decide to keep them, you'll pay only $1.95* per book. And $1.95 per book is all you pay! There is *no* charge for shipping and handling. There are no hidden extras.

4. When you subscribe to Silhouette Books, we'll also send you additional free gifts from time to time, as well as our newsletter.

5. You must be completely satisfied. You may cancel at any time simply by writing "cancel" on your statement or returning a shipment of books to us at our cost.

*Terms and prices subject to change without notice.

Hunter's mahogany eyes locked with Deni's. So much for carefully laid plans, she thought ruefully, trying to return that intense stare. "Not yet. Lacy, would you mind getting my slippers for me? They're by the bed."

Lacy hesitated for just a moment and then giggled. "Oh, I get it. You want to talk in private. Why didn't you just say so?" She whirled around, her platinum curls suddenly airborne. "Call me if he gets violent," she called as she sped down the hall.

A long, uncomfortable silence followed Lacy's breezy departure. Hunter's accusing gaze never waivered, and Deni found herself squirming like a guilty child.

"What's up?"

The question was abrupt, demanding the truth and leaving no room for tactful replies. Deni sat up straighter in the chair, picking nervously at a curled corner of newspaper in front of her. "Since neither Lacy nor I could sleep last night, we had a little talk. She suspected there was something about her dad you weren't telling her and asked me if I knew what it was. I told her about the marriage. We discussed the fact that she couldn't go back home and live alone."

"And?"

"And we decided it would be better for all concerned if she lived with me instead of you."

Deni had steeled herself for an explosion, but it never came. Instead a long silence greeted her announcement. Curious at the unexpectedly calm reaction, Deni risked a peek at Hunter. He stared absently at her, his face speculative. He seemed to be seriously considering what she had said.

"You'd take on a seventeen-year-old?" he questioned.

Deni shrugged. "This particular seventeen-year-old, yes."

"Why?" He moved over to the table, taking the chair next to hers. The smell of coffee clung to him, mingling with his spicy after-shave. That scent should be bottled, Deni thought, unconsciously inhaling deeply. It should be bottled and labeled *Temptation*.

"Deni," he repeated, when she didn't reply. "Why are you willing to take on this particular teenager?"

"Two reasons," Deni admitted quite simply. "First, I care about her."

"But you just met."

"You can care about someone you just met."

He leaned toward her, his face solemn. "You can for a fact," he agreed, lightly tracing her flushed cheek with his fingers. Deni refused to let herself think about the implications of his reply. "And what's the other reason?"

"I want a chance to get to know both her and her big brother better."

He smiled at that, a dazzling smile that took her breath. "No kidding?"

She smiled back. "No kidding."

"We never had our date, Deni."

"But we will," she promised.

"We sure will," he agreed. He got to his feet and began to pace the kitchen. "I'll pay half your rent, of course."

"You will not!" she exclaimed. "This is not a business arrangement. I'm just helping you both—and me—out."

"I won't let her stay unless I pay half your rent," he warned. "And ... I'm going to buy *all* the groceries."

Deni tossed back her hair, irritated by his manipulative manner. "Lacy certainly knew what she was talking about when she said you were bossy."

"I'm bossy, all right," he agreed. "And proud of it. Now there's a little matter of transportation for her. Maybe I can find a car somewhere. Something small, but reliable."

"Would you take a word of advice and let her help you pick it out?" Deni asked.

"Sure. Now is there anything else we need to clear up before Lacy descends on us again?"

"Just one thing," Deni told him.

Hunter raised an eyebrow in silent questioning.

"Lacy and I thought you'd be very difficult to win over. Why are you giving in without a fight?"

Face solemn, he said, "Two reasons. First, I called Roy last night and found out he hasn't even told his new wife he has a daughter."

"Oh, no," Deni exclaimed, her heart going out to her new housemate.

"Not surprisingly he was pleased I'd taken the initiative and moved her. He asked me not to tell her yet. Said he'd be calling her in a day or two himself with definite plans."

"More secrets?" Deni asked sharply.

"What am I supposed to do? Tell her that her dad doesn't have the guts to admit he has a daughter alive and well and worried to death about him?"

"No, you can't do that. It would break her heart." Deni got to her feet, too, walking over to put her arms around Hunter, impulsively hugging him. He looked so miserable—so lost. "Don't worry," she found herself saying when he hugged her right back. "Everything will work out."

"I just don't want her to get hurt," Hunter said.

"We'll make sure she doesn't," Deni assured him. "We won't say anything right now and, if her dad loves her as much as he says, in time he'll come through." At Hunter's dubious look, she added, "I'm sure of it. Now what's your other reason for not arguing?"

"I like your idea about getting to know Lacy's big brother better."

"Oh, you do, do you?" Deni teased, pleased to see a smile playing at the corners of his mouth.

"Uh-huh, and that's because he wants to get to know you better, too. Now I've got Lacy's stuff in Cole's truck. Why don't we round her up and start unloading?"

"You've already been to Tyler this morning?"

"Yep."

"Aren't you clever?"

"I think so," he told her, that hint of a smile now a full-fledged and disgustingly smug grin.

"Hey," Hunter protested less than an hour later when Deni piled yet another shoe box on the stack he held. He couldn't see where he was going as it was. Peering around his armload, he glanced up at Deni, who was standing in the bed of the pickup truck. "Don't you think twenty at a time is enough?"

"There are just two more. Where did she get all these anyway?"

"Heck if I know. She's always been a pack rat. I think she's saved every pair she's ever owned, even if they don't fit anymore."

"There, that's the last one. Lacy's room is the third on the left."

"Right," he responded automatically, juggling his load.

Somehow Hunter made his way into the house, through the kitchen and down the hall. He walked slowly, nearly dropping his burden when Lacy danced past him on her way outside to help. Hunter grinned, enjoying her unusual display of little-girl excitement. Deni was going to be good for little sis, he decided. She was the feminine influence Lacy had lost when their mother had died. Deni would be good for him, too, of course—softening his rough edges, buffering his admittedly caustic tongue.

He leaned back slightly from his boxes, trying in vain to see around them. Had Deni said third door, or third room? he wondered in irritation. He could not remember. He did know it wasn't the closet he'd just discovered or the room he'd just walked into—a dainty bathroom decorated in shades of peach and mint.

With difficulty, he backed out of that room and headed down the hall. This next one must be it, he decided, dropping two boxes when he ran into a closed door. He fumbled for the knob, nearly falling flat on his face when the door swung open unexpectedly. With relief, he eased his bundle to the floor and straightened back up. He glanced around the room, surprised. This wasn't a bedroom at all, but an office—no, an art studio.

Intrigued, he walked over to the drawing table. On it lay an art pad and what looked like a hastily sketched dress design. The dress was stylish, unique, and had a distinct western look about it. Even to his amateur eye it was perfect for Heart Rustler. Without hesitation, Hunter reached for the phone sitting beside the table.

He dialed a familiar number and then waited, tapping his toe impatiently until someone answered.

"Chuck? Hunter here."

"Hey, pal," his best friend, Chuck Masterson, responded. "What's cooking?"

"Funny you should ask. I was thinking maybe barbecued ribs, tonight, my place," Hunter responded. "There's someone I want you to meet."

"A female someone?"

"As a matter of fact, yes. Why do you ask?"

"Beats me. Something in your tone of voice, I think. Is this female special?"

Hunter winced at the intuitive guess. Apparently Chuck knew him better than he thought. "She's special, all right. But not for the reason you think. She's a designer. I think she might be perfect for Heart Rustler."

"Hold everything!" Chuck exclaimed. "Mr. *Top Secret* has told someone about Heart Rustler?"

"Uh, I believe I did mention it." A startled silence greeted his reluctant admission. Hunter tried to ignore it, blundering ahead. "Since I had to be sure you and Susan were free tonight, you two are the only ones I've called so far."

"No problem. Just let me know. Is it all right to bring the kids, or do you want me to get a sitter?"

"Bring 'em," Hunter told him, smiling when he thought of Chuck's two-year-old twins. They were brown-eyed and towheaded, a combination Hunter found irresistible. In fact, he hoped to have a couple of kids just like them someday and decided that with Deni's light hair and his own dark eyes it just might be possible.

Where the hell did that come from? he wondered, bobbling the phone when he realized the disconcerting direction his thoughts had taken. It seemed his intentions were not only beyond friendship, but one step into dangerous territory.

With difficulty, he jerked himself back to the present. "What'd you say?"

"I asked what time. Or would you rather call me back?"

"No. I'm pretty sure everyone here will be cooperative. Let's just say seven. If things don't work out, I'll be in touch."

"We'll see you at seven," Chuck told him.

After his friend hung up, Hunter sat in silence for a moment listening to the hum of the dial tone before he gathered his wits together enough to put down the phone. He tried to assess his feelings for Deni, but found he wasn't exactly sure what they were—other than acknowledging the fact that now that she was in his life, he wanted to keep her there.

He picked up several of her designs, scanning them absently and then minutely, his admiration growing. The drawings were good. Damn good. Too good. A small enterprise like Heart Rustler, though successful and growing, might possibly be nothing more than a stepping stone for a person with this kind of talent.

At that thought another emotion—one he couldn't quite label—replaced the admiration, leaving him confused and more than a little uneasy.

Chapter Six

Looks like you could use a little help," Deni commented to Susan Masterson several hours later. At the woman's rueful nod, Deni reached down and scooped up one of the two toddlers who was clinging to their mother's skirt. Smiling her gratitude, Susan picked up the remaining child and collapsed into one of the lawn chairs on Hunter's deck. Deni did the same.

"Thanks," Susan told her, flashing a rather harried smile. "They're always a little shy for the first thirty minutes or so in a strange place. Unfortunately they usually snap right out of it. In no time they'll be all over the yard. Then the fun begins."

Deni laughed and looked down with pleasure at the squirming twin she held. Dressed in yellow overalls and well-scuffed sneakers, the child was identical to her sister. "How on earth do you tell them apart?" Deni had to ask.

"Several ways. Ramona, here, has straight hair; Rachel has curls. Of course, when they're wearing braids, like they are today, you can't tell that. But there are other differences, too, mostly in personality. Ramona has a short fuse and is very territorial. Rachel just goes with the flow."

Deni smiled, brushing back a strand of Rachel's hair, wispy as gossamer, which had escaped from one of the braids. "I used to think I wanted twins," she commented.

"Bite your tongue!" Susan exclaimed in mock horror. Deni laughed as did Lacy, who'd just joined them. Lacy reached for Rachel, who squealed her recognition. Not to be outdone, Ramona threw her arms up, clenching and unclenching her chubby little fists as she vied for equal attention. Obviously loving every minute of it, Lacy took her as well, and with arms laden headed for the bench swing out in the yard.

Susan heaved a sigh of relief. "Lacy has always been so good with the girls the times she's been around them. Maybe now that she's living so close, we can get her to baby-sit some for us."

"Do you live in Mesquite?" Deni asked.

"No, we live in Dallas proper—actually not that far from the office. And speaking of the office reminds me that I owe you an apology. I had no idea you were looking for a job when you came in last Friday. When you wouldn't talk to anyone but the owner, I assumed you were up to no good. I guess that sounds paranoid, but we've had a real security problem lately. Hopefully our troubles will be over now that Hunter has given me permission to sack Paul."

Deni smiled sheepishly. "I owe *you* the apology. I should have stated my business right away. As for paranoia, I can well understand that feeling since that's the very reason I didn't. I was afraid you'd take one look at my rather primitive drawings and toss me out on my ear."

"From what Hunter tells us, you don't have to worry about that," Susan assured her. "He thinks your work is fantastic."

"So he tells me," Deni interjected, glancing fondly toward Hunter. "Frankly, I think he might be a little prejudiced."

"Prejudice is a mild word for what that poor man's feeling, but he's still right about the drawings," Chuck's deep voice teased from behind her. Deni turned, smiling warmly at him. "You've got a lot of raw talent, Deni, and if you're willing to let me show you a few tricks of the trade and how to smooth out the rough edges, I'm sure we can use you at Heart Rustler."

Deni gasped, leaping to her feet and clutching Susan's arm in her excitement. "Are you serious? Me? At Heart Rustler? Just like that?"

Chuck and Susan laughed. "Just like that," he assured her.

"Oh-my-gosh."

Her movement had caught Hunter's eye and he abandoned his task long enough to cross the few yards that separated them.

"I take it we have a new employee," he said, smiling at her.

"Uh-huh," Chuck told him. He turned back to Deni. "I know you have a dress shop and will need to work around that obligation, but I don't foresee any problems. I do a lot of night work so we can—"

"Oh, no, you don't," Hunter interrupted. "I get her nights." When Deni's face turned cherry red, he quickly qualified that astounding announcement with, "That's, uh, the only time I'll get to see her. We're both so busy during the day...." He cleared his throat. "We'll get her some extra help at the shop so she can spend her afternoons at the office."

"Great idea," Deni smoothly interjected, glaring at Hunter. "It'll probably take me a couple of weeks to get the details worked out, and I'll have to run an ad for some part-time help."

"What's all the excitement?" Lacy asked coming up behind her brother. When he turned to acknowledge her presence, she thrust a wiggling Ramona at him. Smiling his delight, Hunter took the precious bundle. Ramona rewarded him with a rather sloppy kiss, which he obviously relished.

"Chuck is taking me on," Deni told her.

"I told you there was nothing to worry about," Lacy replied, grinning. "When do you start?"

"In a couple of weeks. It'll take that long to find someone to help out in the shop after school, which is our busiest time of day. Even though Christy could probably handle things herself most days, I'd hate to leave her in a bind."

"I could come in after school," Lacy volunteered. "You wouldn't even have to pay me."

"But of course I'd pay you," Deni responded, her excitement growing. It seemed her dreams were coming true before her eyes. She looked toward Hunter, her eyebrow raised in silent questioning.

"What about homework?" was his predictable response.

"I'll do it at *home*," Lacy told him.

"So I can expect you next Monday?" Chuck asked.

"If everything goes as planned," Deni qualified. She glanced toward the grill, now shrouded by billows of smoke. "Hunter!" she gasped, grabbing his arm with one hand and pointing with the other.

"Holy Moses!" He deposited Ramona in her mother's arms and loped toward the grill, throwing back the lid to fan the air so he could assess the damage.

Fortunately no harm had been done and the ribs were a delicious addition to the meal they soon enjoyed. It was after ten before the Mastersons left. While Lacy watched television inside the house, Deni helped Hunter clear the picnic table. When the last paper plate and napkin had been rounded up and disposed of, Hunter took Deni's hand, leading her to the bench swing.

The spotlight that lit the deck barely illuminated that shadowy corner of the yard, and Hunter took advantage of the situation. Laying an arm across her shoulders, he stole the kiss he'd been craving for hours. Deni relaxed against him, resting her head on his shoulder.

"Happy?" he asked her, as he raised his head.

"Ecstatic," she replied. "This is a dream come true for me, you know."

"How long have you wanted to be a designer?" Hunter asked softly.

"Years and years. Even back in high school."

"I'm surprised you didn't just trot off to New York and go for it. Most of the really big companies are there, you know."

Deni laughed. "I can't afford to go to New York. Besides, I've got a lot to learn. Heart Rustler is perfect for me and I'm very excited."

For a few moments the only sound they could hear was the melodic croak of the tree frogs and the creak of the swing as it swayed back and forth. Then Hunter asked, "What do you think of Chuck and Susan?"

"I like Chuck and Susan," Deni replied, adding, "and Ramona, *and* Rachel. In fact I'd like to take those two sweethearts home with me."

"There are days when Susan would let you," Hunter assured her, grinning. "So you like kids?"

"I love kids."

"Good."

Deni turned her head at that cryptic comment, perusing his solemn face. "Do you like kids?"

"Love 'em," Hunter told her.

"Good."

Hunter chuckled. There was another companionable silence before he asked, "Do you like the ranch?"

"I love the ranch. There are just a few things I'd change."

"Yeah?" he asked, leaning back slightly to get a better look at her. "What things?"

"That oak tree over there needs a bag swing. A duck pond would be nice and you could use a small garden spot—for tomatoes."

Hunter laughed. "Miss those things, do you?"

"As a matter of fact I do."

"Tell me about your childhood, Deni," he urged.

Deni sighed. "I had a happy childhood actually. I was content with rural life at that point, didn't mind the hard work because I'd never known anything different. Then when I was fourteen, I spent a summer with my cousin Erica in Memphis, Tennessee. My uncle, her dad, had a white-collar job and their lives were so very different from mine. Although I was glad to get home, I was decidedly restless from that point on. I realized I could choose what kind of life I wanted. I knew I'd never be happy toiling in the sun from sunup to sunset."

"Is that why you married your cowboy? To get away?"

"Exactly," Deni told him, nodding mournfully.

"And is that why you don't get along with your parents?"

Deni nodded again. "That's part of it, I guess. They actually expected me to move back home when I divorced Keith. I didn't, of course. I had a dream."

"You can hardly blame them for wanting you back home," Hunter mused. "You were very young, you know, and an occupation like designer must have seemed rather insecure to them."

"I know, and the older I get, the more I can understand their reasons for hassling me about the likelihood of ever achieving my dreams."

"They hassled you?"

Deni shrugged. "It seemed like it then. Every time I made a visit home they talked about how great Stu was doing—"

"Stu?"

"My big brother."

"Ahh," Hunter said. "Don't tell me, let me guess. Stu's married to a sweet little homemaker. They have two perfect children, a well-behaved dog and a farm within walking distance of your parents."

Deni gaped at him. "How on earth did you know?"

Hunter smiled sympathetically. "Lucky guess." He took a deep breath and ventured, "Don't you think it's time you tried to see things from your parents' point of view?"

"Whose side are you on?" Deni exclaimed, taking his arm off her shoulder and dropping it unceremoniously in his lap.

He put it right back where it had been, tugging her even closer. "As a friend who wants to be more, I have to say something."

"'Wants to be more'?"

"Yes, and don't change the subject. Did you ever at any time feel that if you got into dire straits you couldn't go home?"

"Oh, no," Deni replied. "My parents have always been there for me. They even offered to help pay for me to go to college after the divorce."

"But you wouldn't let them."

"Of course not," Deni told him. "I'd officially left the nest and failed miserably doing it. I had to live with my mistakes; I couldn't go back."

Hunter shook his head. "Deni, Deni, Deni," he murmured.

"What? What? What?" she retorted.

"Has it ever occurred to you that the problems you have with your parents are mostly in your head?"

"That's ridiculous."

"Is it? Have your parents ever told you they think you're a failure?"

"Not in so many words, but they keep throwing Stu up in my face. I'm no idiot." She eased out of his embrace and walked across the yard to a rail fence and a rosebush that she'd noted earlier. The blooms, now barely visible, were still exquisite—velvety soft and perfectly formed.

"That's a matter of opinion," said Hunter, who'd followed her.

Deni whirled around to face him. "You've got a lot of room to criticize my relations with my parents."

Hunter nudged a clump of dirt with the toe of his boot. "Yeah," he agreed. "I guess you're right. I made as big a mess of my life as you did."

"*And*, according to Lacy, broke your mother's heart."

"Lacy was too little to know what was going on when I left, and as for Mother, she made her choice. It was Roy or me, and she chose Roy."

"You mean she actually *told* you that?" Deni asked, aghast.

"Not exactly," Hunter hedged, clearly uncomfortable now that he was the subject of the conversation. "But it was clear to me who she loved best. Besides, she always took his side when we got into it."

"Is Roy a big man, like you?" Deni asked, bending down to smell the blossom she'd cradled with her hand.

"Roy's a shrimp."

"So if you two had actually come to blows, you could have hurt him?"

Hunter winced. "I-I expect so."

"And then gone to jail?"

"Most likely."

Deni shook her head. "Hunter, Hunter, Hunter."

He actually chuckled, echoing her earlier response. "What? What? What?"

"Maybe I'm not the only idiot here."

"That has occurred to me, but it's too late to make amends now. What about you? Are you going to bury the hatchet and go home for Thanksgiving?"

"I'll think about it," she promised. "And it's not really too late for you, Cowboy. You could make Lacy's life a lot more tolerable if you'd try to get along with Roy."

"I'll think about it," Hunter promised.

Their gazes locked. Slowly Hunter leaned toward Deni, kissing her gently, only their lips touching. When he raised his head, she smiled, suddenly feeling closer to him than she'd ever felt to any man before.

"Something's happening here," she murmured.

"Yes."

"I'm not sure what it is."

"Neither am I," he said. "But I have a pretty good idea and, frankly, it—"

"Scares the hell out of you?" Deni teased. When Hunter nodded, she stepped forward, wrapping her arms around his waist, brazenly raising her face for another kiss. He accepted her invitation, covering her lips with his. His tongue teased, tantalized, and she opened her mouth to his exploration.

His hands were never still, tracing lazy circles on her back, cupping her hips to hold her closer, and it was several thudding heartbeats later before he trailed his lips across her cheek.

"Maybe scared isn't what I'm feeling at all," he told her, between breathtaking nibbles to her neck.

"Well, it's what I'm feeling," she assured him, though she overcame her fear enough to tilt her head so he could better reach an especially sensitive area.

"If I'm frightening you, we'd better go in," he murmured huskily, his face nuzzling hers as he drank in the hypnotizing scent of the jasmine she wore.

"I suppose we should," Deni agreed absently.

"Or we could stay and face our fears together," he said.

"Talked me into it."

Hunter groaned softly at her reply, lowering his head once more. Lost in time, they clung together, their troubled pasts and present fears forgotten for the moment.

Four days later, Hunter sat at the seldom-used oak desk in his Dallas office, staring blankly at the résumés of prospective marketing reps that Susan had handed him minutes before.

"Well?" she prompted. "Anyone catch your eye? It would save me a lot of heartache if you could make a decision from these résumés that were left over from the last time we advertised the job. I did a little phoning today and these five applicants are still interested and fairly evenly matched as far as qualifications go."

Hunter did not respond, lost in thought. Ever since those magical moments he'd spent in Deni's arms Sunday night, he'd had trouble concentrating. He had a sneaking suspicion why.

"Yoo-hoo," she teased. "Are you in there?"

"What?" Hunter looked up at her, frowning. "Did you say something?"

Susan sighed dramatically. She sat down on the edge of the desk and crossed her arms over her waist. "Where have you been the past few days? I had a heck of a time reaching you."

"Taking care of Lacy's business," Hunter told her. He straightened in the chair and tried to focus his eyes on the pages in front of him. "Let's see here. This one looks good."

His brunette office manager glanced at the paper he indicated. "Well, he was my least favorite of the bunch, but if you want him—"

Hunter hastily shook his head. "I don't. What about this one?" He picked up the next résumé in the stack.

"Have you read that one?"

Hunter flashed her a sheepish grin. "No."

Frowning, Susan took the paper from him and lay it on top of the others. "Why didn't you just tell me you didn't want to do this tonight?"

Hunter leaned back in the chair and rubbed his eyes wearily. "I'm sorry. I realize I'm making your life difficult. I know you stayed in town just so we could get this marketing rep hired, and I know you have a family at home waiting for their dinner. I just can't seem to concentrate."

"That's what love will do for you."

Hunter started. "Excuse me?"

"That's what love will do for you," she repeated, the beginnings of a smile lighting her eyes. "You *are* in love with Deni, aren't you?"

"What makes you say that?"

"Your distraction, agitation and confusion, that's what," she told him matter-of-factly.

Hunter swallowed hard, his thoughts bouncing around inside his head. Was his suspicion right after all. Was he in love—after seven days? Surely not. "I'm not in love."

"Whatever you say. Now why don't you take these home and read them tonight?"

"Do you think I'm in love?"

Susan grinned at his question. "Do you?"

"Naw," he assured her, taking the folders and getting to his feet.

"You'll call me after you've looked them over?"

"What if I am?"

Susan threw back her head and laughed outright. "Go to the woman you love and tell her."

"I can't do that. What if she doesn't love me back?"

"What if she does?"

He assessed that question in silence for a moment and then grinned. "Yeah. What if she does?"

Susan got to her feet and walked to the door, unnoticed by her boss. She shook her head, biting her lip to keep from laughing again. "Call me, okay? I want to know how you're making out."

Hunter looked up at her, frowning his confusion. "With the résumés?"

"No, doofus. With *your* heart rustler."

Impatiently Deni turned her wayward thoughts back to the task at hand: checking a new shipment of dresses. It was five-twenty on a Thursday and if she didn't want to spend the rest of the night in the shop, she had to get these new garments out on the racks. Now ironed and on hangers, they were ready to display.

Deni hadn't seen Hunter all week. He'd been busy getting Lacy enrolled in school, buying her a car and somehow squeezing in time to take care of his day-to-day ranching obligations. She missed him terribly—more than she would ever have believed possible—and the intensity of her feelings astonished her.

Deni realized it was high time to assess her feelings for this irresistible cowboy. It wasn't easy; most of the roller-coaster emotions she'd experienced over the past few days were foreign to her. She *did* know she cared deeply about him and readily admitted that she might possibly love him a little. But did he feel the same? On one hand, she sincerely hoped he did. On the other, she was afraid he might. What a mess. Shaking her head ruefully, she grabbed an armful of dresses and started out to the front of the shop where Lacy and Christy waited to help her hang them. Just as she stepped into the shop proper, strong hands caught her shoulders in a bone-crushing grip from behind.

"Boo."

Deni whirled around, her heart leaping with joy at the sight of Hunter's cocky smile. She tossed her load over to Christy and threw her arms around him, oblivious of the consequences of that action, knowing only that she needed a hug badly and she needed it from him. He grunted in surprise, but quickly recovered and pulled her close. His lips found hers unerringly. As always the kiss was magic, transporting her away from worldly quandaries into a heaven of security. She kissed him back eagerly, putting her heart into the caress.

"All right!"

Lacy's gleeful exclamation and subsequent applause brought Deni abruptly to her senses. She released Hunter and tried to step away, but he held her tightly. "Can I take it that you missed me?"

Scarlet-faced, Deni nodded, glancing nervously at Lacy. "Let me go," she whispered. "We've got an audience."

"Hey, you started this," he reminded her.

"And I'm stopping it," she countered.

He released her with a chuckle. "What's all the fuss about? Surely by now Lacy has guessed how we feel about each other."

"You betcha!" Lacy exclaimed, a pleased grin lighting her face.

"May I see you for a moment?" Deni asked quietly, taking Hunter's hand and leading him back to the stockroom. She pushed him through the door and then turned toward the two young women who were watching so avidly. "We'll be right back." Hunter walked over to the worktable and sat on it, crossing his arms over his chest. Deni shut the door and turned to him, taking a deep breath. "I'm so sorry I jumped you. But it's been such a long week and I've missed you so much—"

Hunter leaped off the table and reached for her, but Deni slipped out of his arms. She backed away until her body met one of the floor-to-ceiling shelves lining the room. Hunter took a purposeful stride in her direction. Deni threw up a hand to ward off his advance, her eyes wide in alarm.

"Get away from me. Lacy and Christy are liable to come bursting through that door any minute."

He ignored that, catching hold of the shelf on either side of her, pinning her body to the structure. When she turned to avoid his descending lips, he nibbled her earlobe instead, chuckling when she moaned in response. She inched her fingers, which were splayed against his chest, upward, locking them behind his neck. Her rigid body relaxed in stages, until her soft curves were molded against him. She dipped her head slightly, intercepting his lips which were now on a downward path to her collarbone.

"You've got to stop," she murmured weakly against his mouth. "We're going to get caught."

"So?"

"So I can't afford a one-hour explanation about what we've been doing back here. I have work to do—work that has to be done if I'm going to start at Heart Rustler next week."

"You're starting there next week?"

"I'm going to try," she told him.

"Thank God," he murmured. "Maybe I can risk dropping by sometime so I can actually have a few minutes alone with you. There are definite disadvantages to having a little sister around all the time."

"Not only do you get to keep an eye on her," Deni agreed with a quick nod, "but she gets to keep one on you, too."

"Yeah," he mumbled. "And speaking of time alone, be warned that tomorrow night is mine."

"I'll pencil you in my appointment book," Deni teased.

"Let me loan you something to write with," he countered, reaching into his pocket and actually handing her a pen. "Indelible ink."

Laughing at his foolishness, Deni refused the pen and moved toward the door, Hunter one step behind.

"I think Lacy's happy in Garland, don't you?" Hunter mused when they reached the door.

Deni nodded. "She misses her dad, of course, but she's already made some friends."

"Male or female friends?"

"Both, I hope."

Hunter frowned slightly. "I guess you're right. She does need to get out."

Deni made no reply to that and, together, they returned to the front of the shop. She half expected Lacy to descend upon them with a multitude of questions, but to her surprise, both of her helpers were standing by the door talking to a man holding a cowboy hat. He had his back to her, but Deni recognized the plaid western shirt he was wearing.

"Seth?" she called, weaving her way through the maze of racks and tables dotting the store.

Her cousin turned, flashing that familiar grin of his. Deni's eyes widened in pleasure as her gaze swept him. Now here was the Seth she knew and loved—short hair, sharply creased jeans and good old cowboy boots.

"Hi, Deni," he said.

"You aren't in here to lecture me some more, are you?" she asked. Hunter, who was right behind her, hooked a finger through one of the belt loops on her skirt, a gesture that Deni found oddly comforting.

"Naw," Seth murmured. "I was in the neighborhood, and..." At Deni's dubious look, he abandoned that unlikely excuse and laughed. "Actually I was through with classes for the afternoon and since I hadn't seen you for a while, I thought I'd just drive up."

"I see," Deni replied, noting the way his eyes never left Lacy.

Seth flushed at her caustic tone, something she'd never seen him do before. "All right. I admit it. I had another motive. I seem to have acquired two tickets to go see Dwight Yoakam tomorrow night, and since Lacy is new in town and doesn't know all that many people, I thought she might want to go with me." He turned to the blonde. "Would you like to?"

Deni bit back a grin when she felt Hunter's start of surprise. She leaned back slightly, maliciously whispering, "It seems what goes around, comes around." He didn't find that funny. Openly smiling now, Deni glanced toward Lacy, who didn't respond immediately.

Instead her wide eyes took in the measure of the male before her. She glanced thoughtfully at her brother, who was obviously holding his peace with difficulty, and then back to Seth.

"Thank you. I'd love to go."

"Just a doggone minute!" Hunter exploded, stepping between his sister and Seth. "You haven't asked me yet if you can, and I'm not sure this is such a good idea."

When Lacy and Seth both automatically looked to Deni for help, she squared her shoulders, prepared to do battle if that's what it took. "I thought you just said you wanted her to go out more."

"Well, yeah, I did, but I didn't mean with *him*," Hunter responded, glancing disapprovingly at Deni's cousin.

Seth opened his mouth to respond to that, but before he could, Deni did it for him. "What's wrong with *him*?" she demanded, hands on hips. "He's a Hadley, you know. And you're going out with one yourself tomorrow night."

"I realize that."

"So Seth can take Lacy to the concert?"

"No."

Lacy snorted her exasperation, throwing up her hands. "I told you he was bossy," she reminded Deni, adding to Seth, "Are you anyone's big brother?"

Seth grinned. "Nope."

"Good!" Lacy replied.

"I'm not bossy," Hunter protested. "I'm just cautious. Seth's older than Lacy—"

"A year," Deni interjected.

Hunter ignored that. "And he's in college. How do I know I can trust him?"

"Easy," Deni told him, stepping close enough to place her hands on Hunter's shoulders. "The cowboy hat."

"Excuse me?" Hunter asked, frowning.

Deni swayed toward him, letting her body brush his ever so lightly. "If there's anything I've learned from this rather, um, interesting association with you, it's that there are some cowboys you can trust. I believe that you're one, and I *know* Seth is."

Chapter Seven

Hunter's shoulders slumped in defeat. He glanced at Lacy and Seth, both watching hopefully. "Aw, what the heck. She can go."

"Thanks," Seth and Lacy chorused, both grinning broadly. They talked for a few more minutes, working out the details, and Hunter monitored every word. Then Seth left, looking quite pleased with the way things had gone.

Since it was after six by that time, Deni locked the front door and Christy, who had a night class, left immediately by the back exit, which was near her car.

"It's getting dark," Hunter cautioned Lacy and Deni. "Hadn't you two better get on home?"

"Not me," Deni told him. "I've got work to do, remember?"

"May I stay and help?" Lacy asked hopefully.

"You don't have any homework?" Hunter interjected.

"Well, yes I do, but—"

"Go do your homework," he told her.

"But it's not fair for Deni to have to work here alone," Lacy argued.

"I'll help her," he responded, surprising even himself.

Lacy looked from her brother to Deni and then back to her brother. A sigh of exasperation escaped her lips. "I told you before, if you two want to be alone, just say so."

"We want to be alone," Hunter instantly complied.

Lacy grinned. "I'm gone," she said. In two minutes, she'd scooped up her purse and was out the back.

"Wasn't that a little bit obvious?" Deni asked, turning the dead bolt on the door. She was very aware that she and Hunter were now standing in the stockroom, virtually interruption proof for the first time in days.

"The act of a desperate man," he informed her, relaxing visibly, opening his arms. She went to him without hesitation, accepting his hug.

"Thanks for letting Lacy go with Seth tomorrow night. You won't regret it."

"That remains to be seen," he retorted.

"Relax," Deni reassured him, her head nestled under his chin. "Seth can take care of himself and Lacy, too, if necessary. And don't worry about his character. He was valedictorian of his senior class in high school last year, not to mention a finalist in the National High School Rodeo. That last piece of trivia, if anything, should make things right with a cowpoke like you."

"Are you telling me the truth?" Hunter leaned back slightly so he could read Deni's expression. She released him, her face solemn as she x'd her heart with a forefinger.

"Cross my heart."

Chuckling softly, he pulled her into his arms again. "You Hadleys are just full of surprises, aren't you? And speaking of surprises, were you telling the truth a while ago? About trusting me?"

"Uh-huh," she mumbled against his thudding heart. "In fact last Saturday I told Seth I'd trust you with my life."

She could tell that pleased him. "Last Saturday, huh? And what about your heart?" he asked, unknowingly echoing Seth's own response to her declaration.

Deni heaved a sigh, realizing the response she'd made to her cousin was no longer appropriate. "I'm not so sure about that." She traced his firm jawline with her fingers and then pressed feather kisses to his throat and chin. The pulse in his neck quickened beneath her lips, and she chuckled softly in satisfaction.

Hunter growled in reply, a deep, rumbly sound that did things to her own pulse. He matched her kiss for kiss and his hands, which felt warm through the thin fabric of her blouse, began a daring exploration that sent her senses reeling.

"You mustn't," she murmured, catching his eager hands in hers and burying her face in his shirt front, trying to catch her breath. He smelled so good—so wonderfully male. She was weak with wanting him. "We've got work to do."

"Forget that," he told her. "Come home with me. Let's get away from the world for a while."

His invitation enticed her and suddenly she knew without a doubt that she wanted to trust her heart to him. But old fears and insecurities still haunted her, and Deni knew a night of passion would not erase them.

"You know I can't," she told him.

"Why not?" he asked, releasing her. "Don't you like me?"

"Like you?" she asked incredulously. "*Like you?* Oh, Lord."

"May I take that as a 'yes'?"

"A roaring 'yes,'" she assured him dryly.

He grinned in satisfaction. "Good. I like you, too, and now I have another question. Do you *love* me?"

Deni gulped. "Now that's a little tougher," she said. She walked over to the worktable and busied herself with nothing for a minute, gathering her thoughts, refusing to meet his intense gaze. He joined her there, grasping her shoulders and turning her to face him. With his finger, he tilted her head back until their gazes locked.

"I guess I've put you on the spot, haven't I?" he asked. She nodded. "Will it make it any easier if I bare my soul first?" She nodded again. "I've got a feeling—a *strong* feeling—that I'm in love with you."

Relief washed over her, and she sagged against him. "I've got the same feeling." She laughed softly. "We must be crazy; we just met."

"Time has nothing to do with this. Every moment we've been together has been special, and you know it."

"Yes," she agreed. "I *do* know it." She sighed lustily, giving him a wicked grin. "So where do we go from here, cowboy?"

"Good question," he told her, smiling back. "I don't really know for sure, but I'm thinking it might be a good idea if we spent a little time together—got to know each other better." He glanced around the stockroom. "We'll start here—tonight. I want you to tell me everything about this shop of yours. Show me how I can become involved in this part of your life. Tell me how I can help you.''

Deni pointed to a dress rack, which was filled to capacity with garments of all shapes and sizes. ''Well, I have to move those dresses there to the empty racks out front and then sort them by size and style. Then I need to redo the display window. I haven't even decorated for Christmas yet.''

''Then we'd better get busy,'' Hunter said, moving toward the rack, and taking down a double handful of hangers. Deni joined him and in seconds they were engrossed in their task.

She quickly discovered that Hunter was a handy man to have around. Not only was he good at maneuvering heavy loads, but he could reach the sizing markers and tags stored on the top shelf in the stockroom without the step stool. The only bad thing about her male helper was his determination to steal a kiss every time she came within reach. Deni found that habit highly distracting, even though she loved every minute of it. When one quick kiss in the stockroom became two and then three, she pushed him away, finger combed her tousled hair, and exploded. ''We're not getting anywhere.''

''I'm not so sure,'' he teased. ''I thought I was doing pretty good.''

Deni sighed her exasperation. He *was* doing pretty good. So good, in fact, that she was more than a little tempted to take him up on his offer to escape to the ranch and forget about the task at hand.

''I have *just* the job for you,'' she told him impulsively, careful to stay just far enough away so that he couldn't grab her again.

''Oh, yeah?'' he asked suspiciously. ''What's that?''

"Follow me." She led him to the front of the store. There she opened the gate of a head-high white picket fence that served as backdrop for the display windows. She pointed inside. "Take everything out of here and vacuum. Then I'll change the clothes on the mannequin."

Hunter nodded his agreement. "All right, but I get to pick out what clothes to put on it."

"Only if I get final approval, and remember some of my customers are respectable little old ladies. Stay out of the lingerie."

Hunter laughed and moved to his task. Gratefully Deni slipped back to the safety of the stockroom and sank down on the old leather chair at the worktable. Being around Hunter—being the object of his constant teasing—was about to get the best of her. She needed five minutes of peace and quiet to cool down and she intended to have them now. She managed three before his loud shout intruded on her solitude.

What now? she wondered, dashing out front again. Hunter stood in the now-empty display area, coughing, his feet lost in a swirl of dust. A quick inspection of her antiquated vacuum cleaner showed Deni that he had done what she'd done a few times herself—hooked the hose up to the wrong end of the canister. Instead of sucking up the dust, he was blowing it.

"For Pete's sake," she yelled over the roar, "turn it off!"

She blinked against the dust and waved her hands, trying to clear the air, now coughing herself.

"Sorry," Hunter muttered with a sheepish grin. "Maybe you'd better stay out here and supervise."

With a sigh of resignation, Deni did just that. In minutes, the vacuum cleaner was working again, cleaning up the mess. Hunter then volunteered to wash down the plate-glass windows on the inside, a task that took another fifteen minutes. While he did that, Deni washed the fence and dusted the overhead lights.

Finally they were ready to put the mannequin back in the window. Half regretting her promise that Hunter could pick out what dress would be displayed, Deni watched with trepidation while he perused the racks. To her surprise, he chose an exquisitely made dress in vivid crimson, perfect for the fast-approaching holiday season.

"Good choice," she commented.

"I have an eye for beauty," he told her, and the gleam in his eye sent a blush to her cheeks.

"Lacy must have one, too," Deni said. "That's the very dress she picked out the first day she came in here."

Hunter frowned at that news. "She can't buy that! The neckline is too low!"

"Have you heard from Roy?" Deni asked, strategically changing the subject.

"No," Hunter responded, successfully sidetracked. "And frankly, I hope I don't. Now that I have Lacy here and settled, I want her to stay. With a little luck, I'll talk her into going to one of the colleges close by when she graduates."

Deni didn't reply to that, sensing Hunter's determination and fully understanding the fierce possessiveness that drove him. With his unhappy background he would naturally cling to those he loved. But his love could become smothering, and having been on the receiving end of such affection before, Deni hoped that he wouldn't alienate Lacy as her parents had alienated her. She silently vowed to do her best to teach him that love sometimes meant faith—faith that if he allowed Lacy her wings she just might fly back after she tried them.

One glance at Hunter's grim face told her she had her work cut out for her.

"Oh, this isn't right, either," Deni fumed as she turned this way and that, setting awhirl the polished cotton skirt she wore. Usually she liked the way the padded shoulders and narrow waist of this wine-colored dress set off her trim figure. Tonight, however, nothing seemed to suit her. Deni glanced disappointedly at the bed and the four dresses heaped on it—dresses donned and discarded in record time. What a lot of fuss and bother for a man she *might* love.

Might? She frowned at her reflection in the mirror, knowing full well there was no *might* about it. She was in love—desperately, eternally, hopelessly. Deni sank down on the bed, propping her chin in her palm and her elbow on her knee, lost in thought.

Her past experiences had taught her that love inevitably brought sleepless nights, self-recrimination and misery. Would loving Hunter be any different?

"Aren't you ready yet?"

Deni turned at the sound of Lacy's voice. The blonde was standing in the door, dressed in jeans, boots and a western shirt. Her blue eyes were glowing with excitement, her cheeks were flushed.

Look out, Seth, Deni thought, smiling to herself. She got to her feet. "Almost. How do I look?"

Lacy glanced at the pile of dresses on the bed and grimaced. "You look gorgeous, but then I liked the blue one, and the pink one, and—"

"Never mind," Deni told her, ushering her out the door and into the kitchen.

"How do *I* look?" Lacy asked.

"Fantastic." Deni assured her. "You're going to knock Seth's socks off!"

Lacy giggled. "Better not let Hunter hear you say that. He'll go into another one of his 'sit on your side of the car, no parking, keep a quarter in your shoe in case he gets fresh' lectures."

Deni groaned dramatically. "And after hearing that four times already today, I think we'd both rather pass."

At that moment a knock on the door announced the arrival of one of their dates. Deni hurried to open it, smiling when she saw her cousin, hat in hand. She stepped back, letting him into the kitchen. He and Lacy greeted each other shyly and then stood in awkward silence.

"Well, here we are," Deni said, perhaps a little too heartily, but then she was trying not to laugh. How well she remembered those painful teenage days. She wouldn't go through them again for anything. She preferred a mature relationship, like the one in which she and Hunter were presently involved.

Mature? Ha! So far they'd deceived each other, necked on a bench swing in the dark and vowed maybe-love after only seven days. Some mature relationship.

"Here we are," Lacy echoed. "But I'd rather be somewhere else." She turned to Seth. "Do you think we could hurry up and leave before my brother gets here?"

Seth nodded eagerly. "Great idea." To Deni he said, "Tell him I'll have her home by midnight."

When Deni nodded her agreement, the pair slipped out the door, only to collide with Hunter.

"Whoa!" the older man said, halting their escape. "Not so fast. I need to know—"

"I've taken care of everything," Deni assured him, waving the teenagers away. She took Hunter's arm, tugging him into the kitchen and shutting the door behind them. "Lacy can manage. This isn't her first date, you know."

Hunter sighed. "I know. I guess I'm taking this big brother role a little too seriously, huh?"

"Maybe a little, but no one's blaming you. Not even Lacy. Now let's forget about them. This is *our* first real date. I want your undivided attention."

"You've got it, honey," he said, his eyes sweeping her from head to toe. "Ahh, Deni, you make my heart beat like a seventeen-year-old's."

"Thanks, cowboy," she said, adding, "but thank goodness you're not."

He frowned. "Not what?"

"Seventeen."

Hunter laughed at that. "I can only agree with that sentiment. Seventeen was not a good year for me."

"Or me," Deni agreed.

Hunter reached out, pulling Deni into his waiting arms and kissing her. "I've been thinking about our conversation last night," he said when he raised his head, "and I've come to realize I wasn't totally honest with you."

Deni stiffened. "What do you mean?"

"I was wrong when I said I thought I might be in love with you." Startled, Deni tried to slip out of his embrace. He wouldn't let her. "I *know* I am."

She sagged in relief, pressing her weight against him, resting her head on his chest. "I love you, too."

When he didn't respond to that immediately, she raised her head again. Their gazes locked, and Deni was startled to see that his eyes looked suspiciously moist.

"What's wrong?" she asked.

He didn't reply for a moment, merely shaking his head, swallowing hard. Then he drew a shaky breath and said. "I was hoping that's what you'd say, but deep down inside, I guess I never believed you would."

"Why?"

He held her close, stroking her hair before he placed a quick kiss on the top of her head and let her go. "I'm a little shaky where relationships are concerned."

Deni reached up, brushing back an errant strand of his rich black hair. "We're just going to have to relax, talk out our insecurities and take this romance one slow step at a time."

"All right," he agreed easily, adding, "how does a December wedding sound?"

Deni twisted free, gaping at him, heart hammering wildly. "Wedding? Did you say *wedding*?"

"That is where two people in love eventually wind up," he assured her. He frowned. "Don't you want to marry me?"

Deni plopped down onto one of the nearby kitchen chairs, thinking hard about his question. Did she want to marry Hunter Nash? She wanted him, for sure—in her bed and in her life. She wanted to have his children. She'd never felt that way about any other man.

She also wanted to share with him the joy of her work, knowing instinctively that joy would be multiplied if Hunter were involved.

"Deni?"

Jerked back to the present by Hunter's hesitant voice, Deni looked up.

"You don't want to move to the country. That's what's wrong, isn't it?"

Deni thought about his ranch, knowing she would gladly live there just to be on the receiving end of his teasing, his sexy smile and his devastating kisses. She might even be able to tolerate a chicken or two, though she would certainly draw the line at the tobacco. "I'd love to live on your ranch," she told him and meant it.

"You wouldn't want Lacy to live with us? Is that what's bothering you?"

"Don't be silly," she scolded.

He was silent for a minute, clearly lost in speculation. "You love me, but not enough to get married?" he ventured hesitantly.

"No, no, no," she responded hastily, leaping to her feet, hugging him hard. "You just caught me by surprise and you're not the only one who's had trouble with relationships. I figured we'd date for a while, get to know each other better, before we even thought about a wedding."

It was Hunter's turn to sit, his crestfallen expression revealing his disappointment. "How long is 'a while'?"

Deni shrugged. "I don't know. Whatever it takes for me to lay a few ghosts to rest, I guess."

"Are you still comparing me with Keith?" Hunter demanded.

"I don't think so, but I have to admit the thought of getting married again *is* rather alarming," she admitted, walking over to sit on his knee. He put his arms around her, holding her securely. "And there's the little matter of my parents. I've been thinking about what you said—about all my problems being in my head. I've decided you just might be right, and I'd really like to get my differences with them sorted out before I take on the challenge of a new relationship." She leaned forward, kissing him. "Does this make any sense at all?"

He nodded solemnly. "Oddly enough, it does. But don't be surprised if I try to hurry up your decision. I'm not noted for my patience." He glanced at his watch. "It's after seven and our reservation is for seven-thirty. We'd better go."

Obligingly Deni slid off his knee. She watched as Hunter stood, her eyes taking in his dark suit and vest, dress shirt and silk tie. *Mr. Perfect in a three-piece-suit,* she thought, smiling as she remembered her earlier criteria for the ideal mate. How foolish she'd been to let yesterday's fears and insecurities influence her tomorrows. But it wasn't easy to go forward when haunted by past failures.

Maybe she would go home for Thanksgiving, she mused, knowing it was time to face her parents, as Hunter had suggested. Then when she had her troubled teenage years in perspective, she would return to Texas, secure, ghost free and finally ready for all the love this handsome cowboy had to give.

Dinner was everything Deni hoped it would be. Hunter took her to a restaurant in Dallas where they ate by candlelight, a romantic experience they both enjoyed. Since Hunter had promised his aunt and uncle he would bring Deni out to see them, they went to Mesquite after their meal, stopping first at the ranch so that Hunter could outline a few modifications he intended to make in anticipation of the time they would live there together. Disclaiming any desire to rush Deni, Hunter nonetheless walked her through every inch of the house as he talked, strategically concluding the tour in the master bedroom.

"I thought I'd leave this area pretty much as is," he told her, covertly gauging her reaction to his ideas. "I might get rid of the king-size bed, but—"

"Why?" Deni demanded. "It's a magnificent piece of furniture."

"Too big," he told her, sitting on the edge of the quilted coverlet. He patted the mattress beside him and she walked over, sitting down where he indicated.

"Too big?"

He put his arms around her, kissing her before he nodded. "Uh-huh, I'd like to be able to find you if I wake up during the night . . . wanting."

Deni closed her eyes for just one moment, relishing that tempting scenario. When she opened them again, Hunter was grinning at her.

"You're not playing fair," she complained.

"I never do," he admitted.

"I have to go home and work things out with my parents before I can commit myself."

"When are you going?" he asked, his hand cupping her cheek and then slipping lower to push her dress aside and brush across her collarbone.

"Soon," she told him, deliberately avoiding an admission that she'd practically made up her mind on that issue already. She liked his form of persuasion.

"How soon?" His lips had replaced his fingers, which had now slipped even lower and were intent on unfastening her dress. When the garment was unbuttoned, Hunter slipped one hand inside, gently cupping her breast.

"Very soon," she gasped, falling back on the bed, reveling in his touch. He lay beside her and once more his lips replaced his fingers, teasing first one breast and then the other.

"Thanksgiving?" he persisted, raising his head for a moment. His eyes were smoldering and her blood began to boil in response.

"Thanksgiving," she somehow found strength to agree before his lips covered hers. His hands were never still and she answered boldly in kind. "I love you," she murmured, her own fingers finding the buttons of his vest and then shirt. "You're a wonderful man, a good nephew, a dedicated brother...."

Hunter caught her brazen hands in his, groaning softly. "Time to stop."

"Stop! Why?" Deni demanded, sitting up, frowning.

He sat up, too, studiously refastening every button on his shirt and then retucking it, fierce determination on his face. "Just because," was his cryptic reply.

"Well, I never thought you'd tease and not follow through," Deni exclaimed in mock disgust, standing up to rebutton her own garment.

Hunter leaped to his feet at her complaint, catching her up in his arms, pinning her against his thudding heart.

"Would you give me a break here?" he asked. "I just remembered all my warnings to Lacy and realized I'm doing exactly what I hope Seth isn't."

Deni laughed at his candid admission. "That's what I like about you. You're such a honorable, sensible man."

"Honor has nothing to do with it. And if I had any sense at all, I'd never have brought you in here in the first place..." His voice trailed off into silence and they both glanced back at the rumpled bed.

"I think we'd better go see your aunt and uncle," Deni said, looking determinedly away.

He took her arm without hesitation, ushering her toward the door. "And pronto!"

"Where the hell are they?" Hunter exclaimed, looking at his watch for the umpteenth time. Deni automatically glanced at the clock on her kitchen wall, noting it was exactly three minutes since the last time he'd asked that question and only thirty-seven minutes past the time Seth had promised to have Lacy home.

Deni and Hunter had visited with Cole and Hattie until after midnight, and then driven to Garland, certain they'd find Lacy safe at home. But she wasn't.

"They'll be here any minute," Deni assured him. "They probably got caught in traffic or something. You know how congested the coliseum parking lot can get." She stood up, reaching out to catch his arm. "Please sit down and relax."

"How can I relax?" Hunter snapped. "Lacy's my responsibility. I'd never forgive myself if something happened to her while she was in my care."

"She's seventeen years old and one smart cookie," Deni reminded him.

"And she's with an eighteen-year-old who probably drives like a maniac. What if they've run into some kind of trouble?"

"She has a quarter in her shoe just so she can call you."

"But we just got back. What if she's already called and missed us?"

"She'll call again. Now *please* sit down."

He abruptly obeyed, dropping into one of the kitchen chairs where he stayed for a whole eight minutes, drumming his fingers on the table. Then he got up to look out the door one more time and resume his pacing.

When the cuckoo clock in the hall chimed one o'clock several minutes later, Deni silently acknowledged her own misgivings. Seth had promised to have Lacy home by midnight and knew that future dates depended on his keeping that promise. Something terrible must have happened to make him break it.

"That's it!" Hunter exploded. "I'm going to go look for them. You call the police."

"But—"

"Just do it!" He charged for the door, halting abruptly when the phone rang. Hunter grabbed it. "Hello!" Deni saw the relief on his face. "Dammit Lacy, where are you?" There was a silence and then, "What the hell are you doing at Pizza Palace? You were supposed to be back in this house by midnight." He frowned as he listened to what proved to be a rather lengthy explanation. Then he glanced at Deni, a look of remorse on his face. "I know and I'm sorry. We were with Hattie and Cole. Now, I'll be there in a minute. Just stay put." He hung up the phone and turned to Deni, who now stood mere inches away, clutching his arm. "Where on God's green earth is Pizza Palace?"

"A few blocks south of my shop. What's happened?"

"Apparently the concert started almost an hour late and then when it was over, they went with a bunch of Seth's friends to get something to eat. Lacy said Seth figured it would take them exactly fifteen minutes to get here from the restaurant, so they waited until the last moment to leave. Then his car wouldn't start." He slapped the nearby table with his hand. "I knew I shouldn't have let her go out with him!"

"But it's not his fault!" Deni argued, stepping back and reaching for her purse. "His car broke down."

"It might not have if he'd driven something besides that old heap of his."

"That 'heap' is an antique and absolutely immaculate," Deni countered, adding, "and you hardly have room to criticize anyone's mode of transportation anyway."

Hunter blinked in surprise, obviously taken aback. Then, looking slightly shamefaced, he moved toward the door, grumbling, "Well, I'm still holding him responsible. None of this would've happened if he hadn't asked her to go to that damned concert."

Deni stepped in front of him blocking his exit. "If anyone's responsible for this mess, it's *you*. Seth probably wouldn't have asked her out in the first place if a certain, devious cowboy hadn't given him the tickets." When Hunter ignored that remark, she caught his arms, shaking him slightly to get his attention. "I've been on Lacy's end of things so many times, Hunter. I know just how she feels and I'm telling you that you'll accomplish a lot more tonight if you'll just save the lecture until a time when they really deserve it."

"But Deni—"

"Please?" she begged, putting her arms around him, hugging him tightly. Still he hesitated, clearly caught between anger and logic. Sensing she had almost won this latest battle and trying to lighten his mood, Deni tipped her head back and said, "Now, I want you to take five deep breaths and repeat after me: Lacy and Seth are alive and well and haven't done anything wrong. Therefore, I will not yell at them and make a fool of myself."

There was a tense silence. Then Hunter relaxed against her, actually chuckling as he returned her embrace. Grinning, he did as she asked, adding a soft, "Thank God you were here. There's no telling what I might have done," before he released her and stepped out the door and into the night.

Misty-eyed with relief, Deni sagged against the door, mentally echoing his sentiment before heading out to the car. What a headache it was raising a teenager! And Hunter wasn't taking the responsibility lightly. Although usually a levelheaded, reasonably calm man, he had been a nervous wreck—ready to think the worst, accusatory and unforgiving—just like her parents had been when she was that age. It was hard not to lose patience with him, and Deni felt a flash of relief that it was Lacy on the receiving end of his concern and not herself.

She thought back to her parents, to the many volatile encounters she'd had with them. She remembered the times she'd deliberately tested their authority and ruefully acknowledged what a handful she must have been. A feeling similar to remorse washed over her.

How strange and how...encouraging. Maybe that half-hearted promise to go home wasn't such a bad idea after all. Maybe it was time to give the situation a second look with a different attitude.

Chapter Eight

Late the following Monday afternoon, Deni heaved a sigh of satisfaction and looked around the tiny cubicle that was to be her office at Heart Rustler. It was perfect for her. Although small, there was a window that gave her a breathtaking view of Dallas, a large drawing table and enough art supplies to last her the rest of her life. What more could an aspiring designer want?

Chuck had welcomed her warmly, given her an in-depth tour of the suite of rooms that comprised Heart Rustler, and then began outlining a suggested course of training he'd devised with her particular talents in mind. His plans were exciting, but unfortunately he'd had to break off the conversation to take a call from Cyrus Carter, creator of CeeCee Jeans and a designer whose fame rivaled that of Halston and Bill Blass. Awestruck—and more than a little tempted to eavesdrop—Deni had nonetheless retreated to her own office and now sat at her desk waiting for him, her heart thumping with excitement.

How casually Chuck spoke of such world-famous designers. And to think she was going to be a part of that glamorous enterprise. She couldn't belive her sudden good fortune.

For once her life was on an even keel. Not only was she loved by a wonderful man who understood her dreams and was even helping her achieve them, but that same man had taken her advice last Friday night and had acted like a concerned brother instead of a raving maniac when they went to rescue Seth and Lacy. Deni would never forget Lacy's look of grateful surprise or Hunter's whispered "Thanks," on the way home. It seemed he was relaxing a little, learning to trust. Deni cherished that tentative progress.

Now all she needed to make everything perfect was a reconciliation with her parents. She regretted the years she'd spent nursing old wounds. It was time to put the past behind her—to forgive, forget and go forward. Once that was accomplished, Deni felt sure she would have the confidence to give Hunter the commitment he wanted.

"Deni!" Chuck burst into the room and into her thoughts, his face glowing with excitement. "You're not going to believe what's happened!"

"What?" she asked, catching some of his excitement.

"Cyrus has opened a fashion design school in New York. The classes will last six weeks and be taught on a rotating basis by some of the top names in design." Chuck grinned and squared his shoulders, blowing on his fingernails and brushing them lightly across his blue chambray shirt. "One of whom is me, by the way," he bragged, tempering that boast with a little-boy grin. "*And* he's agreed to let you attend for half price since we work together. What do you think? Want to go?"

Deni gasped her delight. "Do I want to go? Are you crazy?" She leaped to her feet, impulsively catching him in a bear hug.

"What the hell's going on here?"

Deni whirled around at the sound of Hunter's harsh demand. She stepped toward where he stood in the doorway and reached out, in her excitement hugging him, too. "I'm going to design school. Six weeks in New York. Isn't it wonderful?"

But apparently it wasn't wonderful—at least not to Hunter, who stiffened in shock. "You're not going to New York," he stated flatly.

At his unexpected response, Chuck and Deni both gaped at him. Chuck recovered first, murmuring, "Excuse me," as he backed out of the office, shutting the door firmly behind him.

When they were alone, Deni turned on him. "What do you mean, I'm not going? Of course I am. Chuck can get me in for half price. I'd be crazy not to go."

"You're not going," Hunter told her. "That place isn't safe for a woman alone."

"But Chuck will be there part of the time," Deni argued.

"And that's supposed to reassure me?" he countered sharply, their recent embrace still gnawing at him.

"Hunter Nash!" Deni exploded. "What's the matter with you?"

"Nothing's wrong with *me*," he countered. "It's you. Of all the harebrained ideas.... Six weeks in New York? Damn, Deni. Whatever possessed you to think I'd agree to such a scheme?"

Bristling at his peremptory tone, Deni put her hands on her hips. "And whatever possessed *you* to think I'm asking your permission?"

He caught his breath. "But you said you loved me."

"And I do, but that doesn't mean I've turned my life over to you. I'm past twenty-one, Hunter. I've managed on my own for many years now, and contrary to what you obviously think, am quite capable of making a trip to the big city *and* surviving it."

"So my opinion doesn't count at all."

"Sure it does," she argued. "I'm perfectly willing to hear you out—"

"And change your mind?"

She hesitated and then replied candidly, "I doubt it."

His eyes narrowed in annoyance. "Then there's no use in saying anything else because I'm not changing my mind, either." He turned on his heel and stalked toward the door, yanking it open and then slamming it soundly when he'd stepped through it.

Astounded by his behavior and more than a little angry, Deni dropped into the chair and stared blankly after him. Where did he get off thinking he could talk to her that way? She wasn't his daughter or even his little sister; she was his equal and expected to be treated as such. He had no right to boss her around.

"Are you okay?"

Deni looked up to find the door opened a crack, and both Susan and Chuck peering in at her.

"Of course," she assured them airily, but to her dismay, her eyes filled with tears of frustration, belying her words.

"I've never, ever seen him in such a temper," Susan exclaimed, walking through the door to perch on a table nearby. Chuck joined her there. "He nearly snapped my head off when he came in and then I heard him yelling at you all the way down the hall.''

"He was angry when he came in?" Deni asked, looking up in surprise.

"Uh-huh," Susan told her, nodding.

"Maybe I should go after him," Chuck mused. "To explain things."

"Forget it," Deni countered coldly to hide her threatening tears. "He'd rather believe the worst." Somehow she mustered a smile. "Now I'd like to hear more about this school we're going to. Tell me everything."

Barely an hour later, Deni was speeding down a boulevard on the way to her house. She was oblivious of the Garland scenery that blurred in passing and was barely discernible in the dusky dark. Still upset, she rehashed every word she and Hunter had exchanged. He'd acted like a spoiled child, making demands and never once listening to her side of the issue. He'd treated her just like her parents always had—undermining her career goals, her integrity *and* her intelligence.

Good and angry all over again, Deni pulled into her driveway and parked her car under the carport. She stomped into the house, acknowledged Lacy's presence with a brisk nod and exclaimed, "That brother of yours is undoubtedly the most exasperating, mule-headed, and just plain bossy human being I've ever encountered!"

"So that's it!" Lacy exclaimed from where she stood by the kitchen sink. "You two had a fight. No wonder Hunter was such a bear when he called a minute ago."

"He called?"

"Uh-huh. He's coming by later. He needs to talk to me."

"He's coming by?" Deni squeaked, definitely not up to another encounter tonight.

"Yeah, but don't worry. He said to watch for him. He doesn't want to come in. Now what happened?"

Deni didn't reply for a moment, making a beeline to the refrigerator and extracting a cold cola. She sank down into one of the chairs, popped the top and took a fortifying swallow before she said, "Sometimes I think that man doesn't have a lick of sense. He—" She halted abruptly and gave Lacy a sheepish smile. "Sorry. For a minute I forgot he was your brother. I don't want to insult him."

"Awww, go ahead," Lacy advised, sitting down across from her, propping her chin in her hands. "I do it all the time."

Biting back a smile, Deni related the events of that afternoon.

"He just flew off the handle at the mere mention of the idea."

The blonde sat in silence for a moment, chewing her bottom lip, obviously deep in thought. "Sounds like he's worried you won't come back, doesn't it?"

Deni nodded, thoughtlessly adding, "And why, I can't imagine. He knows I love him."

Lacy gasped. "You do?"

Deni hesitated and then admitted, "I do."

"And he loves you?"

"That's what he tells me," Deni replied.

Lacy squealed with delight, leaping to her feet and engulfing Deni in a quick hug. "No wonder he's acting like such a jerk."

"But Texas is my home," Deni argued. She took another sip of her soft drink. "I've lived here for eight years. I'm not about to move."

"You and I know that," Lacy replied, sitting down again. "But he'll never believe it."

"Probably not," Deni agreed with a lusty sigh. "What am I going to do with that man, Lacy? He's already talking a December wedding, and neither of us is ready for a step like that. This time around I want a relationship built on trust and understanding. Obviously Hunter isn't capable of giving me either of those."

"But he can learn," Lacy argued. "You can teach him. Look how much progress you've made already."

"Progress? You call going off the deep end because I want to make a little trip to New York 'progress'?"

"But think of Friday night. He didn't even yell at Seth and me."

"True."

"So what if it's two steps froward and three steps back every once in a while. He's worth fighting for."

Deni could only agree. "But what if I'm not up to the challenge?" she asked, thinking back over the last few years. "I'm rather inexperienced when it comes to facing my problems, at least where relationships are concerned. I got married to get away from my differences with my parents, and divorced to get away from *that* mess."

"Mmm," Lacy murmured, getting to her feet. "Not a very good track record, is it?" Deni shook her head slowly marveling at how mature Lacy sounded sometimes. She watched in amusement as the blonde began to pace the kitchen, the wheels of conjecture obviously spinning in her brain. Suddenly Lacy halted, whirling around to face her housemate. "You know you're never going to have enough confidence to take on my brother until you go home and make peace with your parents, don't you?''

"That has occurred to me," Deni assured her dryly, biting back a smile.

"So why aren't you packing?" Lacy exclaimed, throwing out her hands in exasperation.

"Because I haven't even called them yet," Deni told her. "What if they don't want to see me?"

"Don't be ridiculous. Seth told me your mother would give anything if you'd come home for Thanksgiving. Call them right now." She walked toward the phone and lifted the receiver, handing it to Deni.

Pure panic gripped Deni's heart. Her stomach knotted with a sudden attack of nerves, which left her nauseous. She handed the phone back to Lacy. "I can't do it yet."

"Why not?"

"I'm . . . scared."

"Scared? Of parents who want you to come home?" Lacy exclaimed incredulously. "You don't know what I'd give to be in your shoes. My mom's dead; my dad doesn't love me anymore."

"Oh, Lacy," Deni exclaimed. "He *does* love you."

"Then why doesn't he call? Eight days I've been here waiting and now Thanksgiving is just around the corner. What am I supposed to do for the holidays? I don't want to go to Aunt Hattie's with Hunter." Her wistful expression tugged at Deni's heart.

"Then why don't you go to Arkansas with me?" Deni impulsively offered, Lacy's words hitting home. How lucky she was to have parents alive and well and more than willing to welcome her home. Maybe it was time to buck up and face them. Maybe it was time to *grow* up.

"Do you mean it?" Lacy exclaimed, her face lighting up.

"Sure I do," Deni told her.

"Oh, thanks, Deni," Lacy said, handing her back the phone and then dancing around the kitchen in her excitement. "I'll be your moral support."

Deni looked down at the receiver in her hand, realizing that she was definitely going to need some. With a finger that trembled noticeably, she punched out her parents' telephone number.

"Hello?"

Deni's heart turned over at the sound of the familiar male voice. "Dad, it's Deni."

"Deni? Long lost daughter of Russell and Faye Hadley?"

Anxiously Deni listened for any hint of censure, but heard none, just the teasing for which he was renowned. She relaxed a little. "The very one. I was wondering if…" She took a deep breath and tried again, still incredibly nervous. "I mean I thought maybe…" Again she halted. She just couldn't do it.

"You know, hon, we were just talking about calling you. Your mom's bought the biggest ol' turkey you ever saw and plans on making a pan of that corn-bread dressing you love. We were kind of hoping you could get away for a day or two and maybe drive up to help us eat it."

Deni blinked back tears of relief that he was making things so simple. A sudden rush of love filled her heart, and momentarily she was speechless.

"I know you're busy with your shop," her dad went on. "And Seth told his mom you had another job, too, but—"

"I'll be there," Deni blurted out. "And I'd like to bring someone with me, if you and Mom don't mind."

"Bring as many guests as you want. This turkey's a real whopper," he responded, his obvious joy lending a husky note to his deep voice.

"Thanks, Dad," Deni murmured, swiping at the tear that had dropped from one of her lashes and was snaking its way down her cheek. "I'll see you late Wednesday."

When she hung up the phone, she turned to Lacy and laughed jubilantly. "I did it! I've been trying to make that phone call for years and now, thanks to you, I actually did it!"

"Why don't we celebrate?" Lacy said. "There's a pizza in the freezer. I'll add a few extra pepperoni, a dab more cheese, maybe a mushroom or two."

"All right," Deni agreed, adding, "What time is your brother coming by?"

"He said after dinner," Lacy replied, stepping toward the freezer compartment of the refrigerator. Deni moved to help, halting when Lacy exclaimed, "No, this is my treat. You go take a shower or something."

"Thanks," Deni replied, smiling with pleasure. "But I think I'll go draw for a while. It relaxes me."

"And you need to relax?" Lacy teased, already busy slicing a pepperoni.

"If I'm going to eat pizza, I do," Deni informed her wryly, putting a hand to her still-fluttery stomach. She padded down the hall, headed for her office and her sketch pad. Usually drawing was wonderful therapy for her frayed nerves—and tonight she needed a little therapy.

She perched on the stool at her drawing table, automatically reaching for a pencil. Her thoughts had been on Hunter ever since he'd stormed out of her office. She wondered what he needed to talk to Lacy about. Such thoughts of Lacy made her smile. She was glad Lacy was going to Houston with her. Just knowing that that bubbly youth would be there to act as a buffer between Deni and her parents was enough to set her troubled mind at ease.

The minutes passed as Deni sketched absently, her mind on the trip home, her dress shop and Heart Rustler. She hummed as she worked, a sound which faded into nothingness when she abruptly realized what—or actually, who—she was drawing: Hunter.

He looked much like he had that afternoon: eyes blazing with anger, eyebrows knitted in a scowl, mouth a grim line of determination. Deni frowned. That wasn't how she wanted to think of him at all. She tore the page out of her sketch pad and wadded it. Concentrating, she drew him again, this time smiling, and with twinkling eyes—the man she loved. She put her heart into her work, gnawing her bottom lip as she sketched.

"Damn!" Hunter exploded several hours later, slamming his hands down on the steering wheel of his ever-faithful truck, which was now en route to Garland. His thoughts were not on his driving, but on the fight he'd had with Deni—still fresh in his mind—and on the hour-long argument he'd had with Roy just before that. Roy had informed him that his new wife knew about Lacy and that he was ready to move his daughter to Tennessee. Anguished by the news—and positive he was about to lose his sister for good—Hunter had pushed his truck to the speed limit all the way to Dallas, certain Deni would know what to do.

Instead he'd found her in the arms of his best friend, babbling about some half-baked scheme to go to a design school for six weeks in New York, of all places—a city with temptations and excitement. Hunter knew without a doubt that Deni would leave Texas and never return. He'd lost her, just as surely as he'd lost his mother—just as surely as he was going to lose Lacy. He should have known better. He should never have lowered his guard and trusted anyone with his heart. It just wasn't worth the pain.

Hunter pulled his truck to a screeching halt in Deni's driveway. He glanced at his watch, noting that it was nearly ten. He'd deliberately delayed his visit, not wanting to break down in front of his sister; the confrontation with Deni had put him at a definite disadvantage, both frustrating and depressing him.

He couldn't believe that just last Friday night he'd actually congratulated himself on his amazing transformation from an unhappy, bitter, insecure rancher to one who was willing to trust his heart. And here he was, back at square one, lonely, and possibly deserving every bit of the misery that now gripped him.

Hunter opened the car door, and drew a shaky breath. Then he squared his shoulders and walked resolutely toward the kitchen door. All he had to do, he reminded himself, was to get Lacy to go for a little drive so that he could tell her about Roy's phone call. He would give her the news, keep his objections to her moving a secret and leave before he revealed his anguish. He wouldn't have to see Deni at all . . . unless she

came to the door. That idea gave him pause, and
Hunter slowed his steps.

He shook his head, marveling at how the mere
thought of facing that petite woman made him trem-
ble, when time and again he'd kept his cool in the path
of a charging bull. Somehow he had to get hold of his
tenuous composure. He wished things had been different. He wished he'd had enough faith in her to discuss
this school thing instead of making unfair demands and
telling her what to do with her life. He was worse than
her parents. She probably hated him; she would certainly never forgive him.

Bewildered and distressed by that idea, Hunter
crossed the last few feet to the house. He ignored the
bell, venting some of his pent-up emotion on the door
as he banged on it with his fist.

Lacy opened it immediately. "It's about time you got
here. I've been worried sick about you. I've called the
ranch at least a dozen times."

"I've been driving around. We need to talk. Want to
go for a little ride?"

Lacy cocked her head, her bright blue eyes appraising her flustered brother. "Why can't we talk here? Now
would be a good chance for you and Deni to try to patch
things up."

Hunter shook his head. "Hell, Lacy, why would she
want to patch things up? She's lucky to be rid of me."

"I don't think she'll agree, bro. She's sure been
moping around the house since she got home." Lacy
shook her head, a look of disgust on her face. "And
you idiots call yourself adults. Some role models you
two are."

He ignored her last comment, that first revelation
cutting him to the quick. It sounded as though Deni was

as miserable as he was. That came as a surprise and he found he wanted to pursue that piece of information. But first things first. With effort he dragged his thoughts back to the chore at hand. "Roy called this afternoon. You and I need to talk."

Lacy's eyes widened. "Let me get a jacket and tell Deni," she said. In minutes they were in Hunter's truck speeding toward the nearest dairy bar.

"Want something to eat?" he asked, when he'd parked the car in a far corner of the lot.

"No, I want to know what Roy said," Lacy replied impatiently.

"Mind if I get something?" Hunter asked, unconsciously postponing the moment he would have to tell her the truth. Roy wanted her in Nashville, even if his new wife didn't. Lacy wanted to go. Soon big brother would be alone . . . again.

"I guess not." Hunter opened his door, and put one foot out on the concrete, freezing when she asked, "Hunter, just tell me this: is he coming home?"

Sick at heart, he put his foot back inside the truck. The time for truth had come. He felt his world crumbling around his feet. First he'd lost Deni and now Lacy was about to leave him, too. Slowly he shook his head. "No. He's decided to settle in Nashville with his new wife and her three kids—"

"Three kids!" Lacy exploded, her eyes widening in shock. "His new wife has children?"

Hunter nodded briefly.

"No wonder he didn't call. He's got his hands full." Lacy turned to her brother, glaring at him as she demanded, "How long have you known this?"

"I swear I just found out about them today," Hunter assured her. He didn't add that he was as shocked as

she and now understood Roy's hesitation to make his
teenage daughter's existence known. "Look, he really
wants you to move up there and I know you're anxious
to join him, so I figured I'd take you Wednesday. That
way you can be with him for Thanksgiving."

To his astonishment, Lacy's expected squeal of joy
didn't come. She didn't even smile. Instead she shook
her head. "Can't go Wednesday. I promised Deni I'd go
home with her. I didn't think you'd mind if I missed one
day of school, and Friday's classes are already can-
celed. We'll probably come back on Saturday."

"So Deni's really going home," he mused. Roy
Beecher's problems suddenly became the last thing on
his mind.

Lacy nodded, a pleased smile on her face. "She's decided that going home to see her parents is a good first
step toward confronting her problems instead of running away from them." Her smile turned into an im-
pish grin. "I think you're one of those problems, by the
way, so if things go well back in Arkansas—and I'm
going to make sure they do—*you'd* better watch out,
Hunter Nash!"

For the first time in hours Hunter's mood lightened.
He could tell that Lacy actually thought there was hope
for him and Deni in spite of the mess he'd made of
things.

"I owe her an apology, you know."

"Yep."

"Maybe I should try to talk to her tonight."

"Great idea," Lacy agreed, reaching out to turn the
key in the ignition before he could change his mind.
Hunter smiled at her ploy and put the truck in gear.

"By the way, how was the Yoakam concert?"

Lacy rolled her expressive blue eyes. "Fan-tastic! I'm surprised you didn't get some tickets yourself, you're such a fan of his."

"Yes, I know," Hunter agreed dryly. "What do you think of Seth?"

"Seth's a nice guy. We're supposed to go to a rodeo together Saturday night with a bunch of his friends if Deni and I get back in time."

"The charity rodeo at the Mesquite Arena?" Hunter asked. Lacy nodded. "Good. I'm going to be there, too. I'll be able to keep an eye on you—at least this time." He gave her a rueful grin, holding up a hand to ward off her arguments. "I know. I know. You can take care of yourself. I forgot." He laughed softly. "I guess you'll be glad to be moving off to Nashville."

"Who says I'm moving to Nashville?"

He turned to look at her, not daring to believe his ears. "You're not moving?"

Lacy shrugged, smiling sheepishly. "Right now I'm not really planning on it. I may go there for a visit, but I'm pretty sure I don't want to live with some strange lady and her little kids. I'd hate to hurt Dad's feelings but, well, I keep thinking how hard your life was after your mother remarried and I—"

"Roy would stand up for you, Lacy," Hunter interjected, knowing it was true.

"I know. But I think I'd rather just stay where I am until school's out and then move out to the ranch with you—if you're willing to put up with me, that is."

Moisture blurred Hunter's vision. He blinked rapidly, unable to speak for a second. So little sis wasn't going to leave him after all. Lacy reached out and swiped at a tear that was snaking down his cheek. He slid an arm around her, holding her tight. His world was almost right again. Almost. "You know I am."

"Thanks, Hunter," she whispered. "I *do* love you."

"I love you, too, honey." There was a long silence and then he pulled away, suddenly suspicious. "Does Seth Hadley have anything to do with this decision?"

Lacy giggled. "Seth and I are just good friends, but he's got a new roommate you might need to worry about."

Hunter digested that in silence and then, still not believing his sudden turn of luck, generously decided not to press it. "And you're really going to move out to the ranch?"

"Yes," she said smiling up at him. Impishly she added, "and just so I don't cramp your style when you and Deni make up, I'll take the bedroom farthest down the hall!"

With a skill borne from years of practice, she dodged her brother's playful fist and in seconds they were headed back to Deni's.

Chapter Nine

Three blocks away from Deni's, Hunter had second thoughts about the wisdom of talking to her. One block later, he lost his nerve entirely and refused to get out of the truck when he stopped it in her driveway. Nothing Lacy said could change his mind.

"But you told me you would," she fussed.

"Everyone's entitled to a moment of insanity now and then," he replied stubbornly. His emotions had run the gamut that day. He felt drained and, in spite of Lacy's astonishing decision to stay in Mesquite, insecure enough to doubt that his happy ending was as imminent as she claimed.

"You're such a coward!" she exploded after she climbed out of the truck. She glared at him from where she stood in the driveway on the passenger side of the vehicle.

"Maybe," he agreed calmly, determined not to let his younger sister shame him into a confrontation he was in no condition to handle. "I'm just not as certain as you are that she's ready to forgive and forget, okay?"

"Oh, all right," Lacy agreed, finally giving in. "Grown-ups," she mumbled as she turned toward the house, shoulders slumped in disappointment. "And I thought seventeen was the pits."

She entered the kitchen and headed down the hall to the lighted bedroom-turned-art-studio where Deni usually worked on her designs. Deni wasn't there and the sound of running water next door told Lacy she must be in the shower.

Lacy walked to the drawing table and sat on the rotating stool in front of it, turning first this way and then that while she waited for Deni. Absently she picked up the drawing pad laying in front of her, starting in surprise when she saw a sketch of her brother.

"Like it?" Deni asked from the doorway minutes later.

"It's magnificent," Lacy exclaimed, her eyes never leaving the drawing.

Deni joined Lacy at the table and wiped her still-damp hands on the chenille robe her mother had sent her last Christmas. She took the pad, trying to see it from someone else's point of view. She'd spent hours on this likeness of the man she loved, putting to paper the feelings she had for him. Every plane and angle was perfection to her own critical eye. Impulsively she tore it out of the sketch book, thrusting it at Lacy. "Here, it's yours."

"You mean I can keep it?" Lacy exclaimed, a bright smile lighting her youthful face.

"Uh-huh."

"Thanks," the teenager gushed, taking the sheet of paper and staring at it with awe. She hesitated a moment, obviously thinking, and then asked, "Would you write something across the top and sign your name?"

Deni chuckled, flattered by Lacy's admiration. "Sure. What do you want me to say?"

"With all my love, from Deni," Lacy replied without hesitation.

"All my love?" Deni questioned, just to be sure she'd heard right.

Lacy nodded solemnly.

Although that message sounded awfully mushy for a seventeen-year-old, Deni good-naturedly complied. She wrote the words with a flourish and then signed her name. Lacy took the picture, hugging it to her body, smiling with pleasure. "Thanks, Deni."

"Don't mention it. Now before I die of curiosity, what did Hunter want to talk to you about?"

Lacy then told her Hunter's news, ending the narrative with her astonishing decision to move to Mesquite. Deni's heart leaped with joy.

"What did your brother say?" she asked.

"He seemed...pleased," Lacy hedged, her misty eyes telling Deni all she needed to know.

Very near tears herself, Deni reached out, pulling Lacy into her arms, hugging her hard. "I'm sure going to miss you."

"But you'll be there, too," Lacy argued.

Deni released her, stepping back to busy herself with straightening her worktable.

"Won't you?" Lacy persisted, catching her arm, frowning worriedly.

"I hope so," Deni told her, with a sad smile. "I sure hope so."

Since Houston, Arkansas, was a good eight-hour drive away, Deni and Lacy left Garland early on

Wednesday. The sunrise was breathtaking that morning, giving Deni hope and a strong feeling that she was right to go home. It was time to put the past behind her—time to face her ghosts and conquer them.

She smiled at the notion that Hunter could be called a ghost. He might be haunting her, but he was no spirit. He was warm—a flesh and blood male whom she wanted in her life. Could she get past her insecurities and go to him someday soon, wholehearted, sure of her feelings, ready to face the challenge of what might prove to be a difficult relationship? Would he ever be able to trust his heart to her, love her even though she didn't always do what he wanted her to do?

She and Lacy ate lunch at a roadside restaurant in Texarkana, Arkansas. She called Seth's mother and father from a pay phone, not at all surprised when her cousin answered the phone himself. He'd told her he was leaving Dallas Tuesday afternoon after classes. Anxious to get home, Deni resisted his pleas that the two of them stop by for a soft drink and quick visit, and in less than an hour, she and Lacy were on the road again.

Lacy had never been to Arkansas before and she was bursting with questions about Deni's home state. Lost in the beauty of the rolling countryside and bright blue skies, she didn't seem to notice that Deni got quieter with every mile that brought her closer to her home. By the time they turned the little car into the gravel driveway of her parents' house, at around four-thirty that afternoon, Deni's stomach was churning with nerves the way it had on Monday night.

She was tempted to turn the car around and make another escape, but she didn't give that idea more than a passing thought. It was time to face her problems—get on with her life. Turning to Lacy, Deni smiled weakly. "Well, this is it. Home."

Lacy looked at the white frame house and grinned. "I like it. Come on, I'm dying to meet your parents." Before she could get out of the car, Deni caught her arm.

"I'm incredibly nervous," Deni admitted.

Lacy nodded solemnly. "I don't blame you; I'd be, too. The trick is to never let them see you sweat. Be the woman you are back in Garland: smart, self-assured, *in control*. You're a responsible adult. You don't have to apologize for being successful at what you love." With that surprisingly sage advice, she bounded out of the car and headed for the porch.

She's right, Deni thought as she followed, much slower. Her parents were standing there, waiting. Deni felt like a stranger, and knew deep inside she had only herself to blame. Her exile, though necessary as far as she was concerned, had definitely been self-imposed. Her parents had never asked her to leave, had wanted her to stay, in fact, but under their terms. Had the years apart changed them as much as they had changed her? she wondered. Could they accept her for what she was now—a career woman of the eighties? Could she accept them for what *they* were—hardworking country folk who seemed, she suddenly realized, as nervous as she.

Deni took a deep breath and gave this reunion all she had, first greeting her mother.

"Hi, Mom," she said, her voice husky with emotion. Then she looked toward her father. "Hi, Dad." Her mother dabbed her eyes with the corner of a crisp, white apron, unable to speak. Her dad didn't have that problem, however.

"About time you came back to see your old man," he scolded. Deni stiffened at his words. Her eyes locked

with his and she realized with a shock that a mischievous twinkle lurked in their gray depths. *Funny,* she
thought. *I'd forgotten about that twinkle.* Suddenly she
remembered other things as well: his dimples, his bushy
white eyebrows, that Kirk Douglas cleft in his chin. She
glanced at her mother, noting that her hair, which was
caught up in a clip, was silvery white and as curly as
ever. Her mother's skin was petal soft, enhanced by her
naturally rosy cheeks. Thank God they were alive and
so healthy, she thought, suddenly realizing that she
could set the tone for this homecoming by remembering the good times and not the bad.

"I've missed you two," Deni said.

Her mother found her tongue. "We've missed you,
too. Now I want to meet your friend."

Deni introduced her housemate, delicately omitting
the fact that Lacy was also the little sister of the man she
loved. Lacy, however, was not so reticent.

"I'm Hunter's sister. I guess Deni's told you all about
him."

"Hunter? No, I don't believe she has," Faye Hadley
replied, her eyes darting to her daughter's flushed face.
"Why don't *you* tell me about him."

Lacy opened her mouth and Deni knew, she was
willing—no, eager—to do just that. "Later," Deni interjected, catching Lacy's arm and pulling her down the
hall to the bedrooms. "I want to unpack and show Lacy
around. Shall I put Lacy in Stu's old room?"

Just as Deni reached her own bedroom, she heard her
mother say, "Yes," and then softly add, "thanks for
coming home, honey."

After they put their suitcases away, Deni went into the
kitchen to see if she could help with the supper she

smelled cooking. Her mother refused her offer, however, advising Deni to let her father show her the improvements he'd made to the farm over the past few years. She hinted that Deni should take pains to be properly impressed, since he was quite proud of what he'd done.

And Deni was, though the changes saddened her just a little, too. The weather-beaten barn where she'd played as a child was no longer there. Instead a much sturdier structure housed the farm equipment. The tin covering that had served as the roof for the old barn was gone, too, replaced by shingles. Remembering all the stormy afternoons she'd lain in the hayloft listening to the drumming rain, Deni wasn't so sure she considered this particular change a real improvement.

There were other differences, as well. Now her parents had city water. The pump house had been turned into a storage area and the walls were lined with shelves that held her mother's canned goods. The storm cellar was still there, buried into the side of the hill in back of the house, but the creaky wooden door had been replaced by a stronger, metal one. Deni remembered the countless times she'd sat in her mother's arms, seeking comfort as they waited out one of the springtime tornadoes for which their area was notorious.

The yard around the house looked much the same, though the trees were taller. Deni noted with pleasure that the bag swing was right where it had always been and suspected Stu's two children probably made use of it now.

"How's Stu?" she asked her father as they walked and looked.

"Fine," he said with a nod. "He and Joyce will be over tomorrow, and the kids, too, of course. They're all anxious to see you."

Deni was anxious to see her brother, too, even though they'd never been as close as she would have liked. Maybe now that they were both adults the seven years between them wouldn't be so hard to bridge. Sometimes she couldn't help but worry about him, hoping that he was really as happy as he appeared to be and wasn't a farmer just because he'd thought it was expected of him.

Russell stepped up onto the front porch when they had finished the tour, reaching out to open the screen door and then waiting for the two women to enter.

"I'll come inside in just a minute," Deni told him, adding to Lacy, "You go on in if you want."

Obviously taking the hint that her friend needed a few moments alone, Lacy complied. Russell followed, shutting the door behind them. Once by herself, Deni sat in the porch swing looking out over the vast front yard, and at the gravel driveway that could be treacherous to a child on a bicycle.

She smiled as she remembered all the wrecks she'd had—at least one a week in the summer—and how her mother never lost patience, fussing over her, bandaging this or that knee after kissing the injury to make it better.

And then, knowing full well that Deni would ignore her advice, her mother suggested that riding on the grass—and slower—might be less painful. Deni laughed softly to herself, now acknowledging that her mother only wanted to save her a little heart—or, in this case, *knee*—ache.

Could it be that all the unwanted advice to which she'd been subjected as a teenager was the same thing—merely an attempt to share the wisdom gained through years of experience, a way of saving her a little agony? Probably, she realized, regretting that she hadn't been more receptive to their words and listened just a little closer. She might never have married Keith, but then she might never have realized her dream to be a dress designer, either.

She knew her parents only wanted what was best for her, but from their point of view. Maybe it was time to prove to them that what *they* thought was best might not have been right for her. Somehow she had to reassure them that though she'd made mistakes along the way, she'd learned from those mistakes and was now happy—or would be, once she got things sorted out with Hunter.

She thought of the last time she saw Hunter, two long days ago. It already seemed like an eternity. How she missed that cocky grin, those flashing eyes. She even missed that fiercely possessive manner of his that was so darned annoying but demonstrated just how much he loved her. She wondered if he would ever *really* understand that even though she had dreams and goals, he would always be the center of her world. She hoped so, but had to acknowledge that he might not. His feelings of insecurity were as deeply ingrained as her own need for independence.

So what are my choices? she asked herself, though she already knew. She could either take on the challenge of Hunter Nash, with all his insecurities, or she could live without him, and be as independent as she pleased.

The thought of never again experiencing one of his breathtaking kisses or discovering if he *could* find her in that king-size bed of his depressed her more than she would ever have believed. Tears welled in her eyes and she knew it was time to fight for what she wanted, even at the risk of losing everything.

The sound of laughter drifted from inside the house, breaking into Deni's reverie. Smiling to herself, she halted the motion of the old swing and got to her feet, drawing a fortifying breath of the clean, country air before she went inside to give those parents of hers an extra hug—one of appreciation and maybe just a little understanding.

Thanksgiving proved to be a busy day for Deni and Lacy. Since they traditionally celebrated the holiday with a noontime get-together, the smells of baking bread and turkey permeated the house early that morning, mingling with the familiar scent of freshly brewed coffee.

Stu, his wife, Joyce, and their children, Sarah, aged seven, and Steven, aged ten, were at the house by nine-thirty. The youngsters were everywhere, immediately dragging a delighted Lacy over to the duck pond she'd only seen in passing the night before.

Although usually reserved, Stu nonetheless hugged the sister he hadn't seen in four years, his pleasure showing in his shy smile of welcome. Deni found an excuse to be alone with him as soon as she could, suggesting he help her retrieve some canned pickles and relishes from the old pump house.

On the way there, she grabbed his hand, dragging him to the privacy of an old oak tree that he used to help her climb so many years ago. Although surprised, he co-operated good-naturedly.

"How are things with you?" Deni asked him, once they were alone.

"Fine," he told her. "Joyce is doing some substitute teaching this year, you know. Steve's playing football; Sarah's in Brownies."

"But how are *you*?" Deni asked again.

He looked surprised by the question. "Okay, I guess. The farm's beginning to make a little money. I'm about to buy another fifty acres—good bottomland."

Deni gave him a long, hard look, suspecting that he really meant what he said; he *was* happy with his life. Not for the first time, she wondered how siblings could be so different.

"And what about you?" he asked softly, kicking a clump of grass at their feet. The gesture told Deni just how uncomfortable he was with their little heart-to-heart chat.

"I'm very happy," she told him. "My shop's doing well and I've got a part-time job as a dress designer."

Stu grinned at that, surprisingly reaching out to tug a lock of her hair in a familiar gesture of affection she'd forgotten. "Mom told me. It looks like all those hours of drawing paper doll dresses are finally paying off."

Deni laughed, remembering the exotic outfits she'd created for those paper dolls. "Yeah."

"Mom's really proud of you," Stu told her. "She brags on you at church all the time."

"She *does*?" Deni asked, surprised.

"Sure she does. It's not every mother whose daughter designs dresses for a company as famous as Heart Rustler."

"You know about Heart Rustler?"

"I may be a poor overworked farmer, Deni," Stu scolded, "but I *do* read the paper on occasion. I've seen the ads."

Deni had to laugh at her naïveté. "Of course you have." She hesitated just a moment before adding, "As for designing dresses, I just started working there this week. I haven't actually contributed anything yet."

"But you will," Stu assured her.

"Oh, yes," she agreed. "I will." She gave her brother a warm smile and glanced toward the house. "I guess we'd better go back, but I have one more question."

Stu grinned. "Just one?" he asked with mock surprise.

Deni graciously ignored that. "How are Mom and Dad? I mean *really*?"

Stu stood in silence for a moment, obviously gathering his thoughts before he spoke. "They're doing well. Dad's thinking about retiring, you know, and Mother's happy doing whatever he wants to do. I think that today they look happier than I've seen them look in years. I believe it's because you're home and I'd be less than honest if I didn't say something that's been on my mind for a long time."

Deni braced herself for his censure, knowing she surely deserved it.

"They love you so much. Could you please not wait so long to come home again? It's hell trying to be everything to them."

His words took her by surprise. So Stu sometimes felt pressured, too. That sudden insight made him seem much more human and did wonders for Deni's morale. Impulsively she threw her arms around him, patting his back in sympathy.

"I'll bet living next door to them gets to be a real drag sometimes," she prompted softly.

"You've got that right," he agreed with a hearty laugh. "No matter what I do, Dad knows a better way. He needs someone besides me to advise. I was thinking if you came home every other weekend—"

"Not every other weekend," she interrupted hastily, grimacing. "But I might make it once every two months or so. That might take some of the pressure off of you. Okay?"

He heaved a sigh and nodded. "Okay."

Back in Texas, things were not going so well. Although Hunter spent the holiday with his aunt and uncle—making a show of smoking the turkey and enjoying every bite of it—he suspected his relatives were not fooled. They offered no protests when he left soon after the meal, walking back home to spend a lonely evening watching the football games on television.

The next day he tried to stay busy, heading out over the vast acres of his ranch to check fences. He was not only alone, but lonely. Near lunchtime he gave up his task, halting the battered vehicle near his catfish pond and sitting in the cab of the truck for over an hour, listening to the radio and watching two squirrels gather acorns on the rocky ground nearby.

He missed Deni badly, and she'd only been gone two days. How would he ever survive her six-week trip to New York, living every minute in fear that she might not be able to resist the lure of the bright lights and the glitter of the fashion design industry that was so firmly rooted there?

He loved her so much and with that intense feeling came a desperate desire to put her under lock and key, keep her by his side forever. Once before he'd experienced the devastation of being rejected by someone he loved. Could he risk his happiness again? What if Deni did as his mother had done—ruthlessly abandoning him to embrace a new life in which he had no place.

Ruthlessly abandoned? He winced, thinking back on what had happened so many years ago and realizing those terms might not be completely accurate. His mother had never exactly abandoned him. He'd been the one to leave. But she'd certainly made it clear whose side she was on.

Or had she? He dug into the shadowy corners of his memory, trying to recall that fateful night when they'd had their last traumatic confrontation.

Roy had been drinking, as usual. He was out of work, irritable and short with Hunter, who had asked to borrow the car for several hours. When Roy had said no, Hunter had then gone to his mother, hoping she would give him the permission he sought—a ruse that always infuriated Roy. Looking back Hunter realized it had put his mother right in the middle.

No doubt sensing they were on the brink of another one of the volatile arguments that had become almost routine, his mother had suggested a compromise. Hunter could have the car for two hours instead of four, a stipulation that wouldn't really cause that many problems since Hunter was just going to meet some friends and do a little cruising.

But Hunter was stubborn—almost as stubborn as his stepfather. Neither intended to compromise and their angry shouts escalated to push and shove. Hunter's mother, trying to soothe a crying Lacy and frightened that someone might actually get hurt this time, stepped between the men, deferring to her husband's violent temper as she pleaded with Hunter to forget the Friday night ritual, just this once.

Taking that as a clear choice on her part, Hunter had stormed to his room, locking the door. He packed everything he owned in a duffel bag left over from his real dad's military days, loaded his billfold with the money he'd been saving to buy a teddy bear that Lacy had cried for one day while shopping and crawled out the window. Several hours and a long bus ride later, his uncle had picked him up at the bus station in Dallas.

Although he'd visited home on several occasions, and kept in close touch via telephone with the little sister he always cherished, Hunter never made any attempt to move back. He blamed that on the fact that his mother, who no doubt enjoyed the peace her rebellious son's absence inevitably brought, had never asked him to. Never mind that he was going to leave home to go to college in another year anyway.

Hunter sighed, absently plucking a tall blade of grass and then chewing on the end of it. He acknowledged that things looked a little different now that he was older and understood the strong ties between a man and woman. He could see that his mother had certainly had her hands full with a resentful teenage son, a toddler and a worthless, but much loved, husband. And maybe if Hunter hadn't been so intent on forcing her to make a choice between the things she held dear, they eventually would've been able to make it as a family.

He just didn't know. He *did* know that while it was certainly too late to make it up to his mother—and probably too late for him and Roy—by the grace of God, he still had Lacy, who meant the world to him. He was going to make the best of their time together, build a relationship that would last forever. And if that meant stepping back and letting her have the freedom to make her own mistakes, then he would just have to do it, no matter what it cost in blood, sweat and tears. Besides, he probably didn't have anything to worry about; she was pretty smart for her age. Hadn't she chosen to live at the ranch instead of with Roy, who would probably be a poor influence on her?

Hunter was still amazed that she'd made that decision. Never in his wildest dreams had he imagined he would get so lucky. That just proved you could never be sure just what another person might do, and *that* made him wonder if maybe, just maybe, Deni might surprise him, too, and come back to Texas after her school-

ing—happier, fulfilled and brimming with ideas for
Heart Rustler.

That possibility made him smile and now that he was
thinking about it clearly, it didn't sound that far-
fetched. She had a good business in Garland. She had
a new job at Heart Rustler. What more could a woman
want?

A little understanding? Trust? Freedom? Was he capable of giving her those things? He thought that with
a little practice he might be, but how on earth was he
going to convince her of that? Would she be willing to
make the effort to see past his grumpy, insecure exterior to the possibilities that existed inside?

It was nearly dark when Hunter drove back to the
ranch, tired, dirty and no closer to peace of mind. He
parked the truck and headed for the mailbox, which
now had a long, tubular package sticking out of it.

Curious, Hunter reached for it, frowning when he
spied Deni's return address. What on earth? he wondered. He waited until he'd cleaned up before opening
the package. Then, comfortable in sweats and a T-shirt
and relaxing in his favorite recliner, he used his pock-
etknife to slice the tape binding it.

Carefully he drew out a rolled-up piece of paper,
which was thick, white and had obviously been torn out
of an art pad. He unfolded the drawing a millimeter at
a time, blinking in surprise when he read the words
scrawled across the top: With all my love, from Deni.

He picked up the pasteboard tubing in which it had
been mailed, noting that the postmark was Tuesday
morning, after their fight. Slowly he unrolled the art
sheet the rest of the way, catching his breath when he
realized what it was—a pencil sketch of himself.
Sketch? No, he acknowledged, more than a little awed,

it was a masterpiece—a work of art. The face of the man before him sparkled with life. He was laughing, the dimples he'd always hated deeply evident. There was a flush on his cheeks, a twinkle in his eye, and Hunter couldn't help but wonder when he'd ever looked that relaxed and happy.

Not since these ups and downs with Lacy, he knew, and not since he'd thought Deni was a reporter or even since he'd realized he was in love and started worrying about losing her. Yet here was a drawing of him at his best. Deni had indeed overlooked the grumpy, insecure exterior he presented every day, and had seen the possibilities that existed inside him.

Suddenly Hunter's heart filled with love and overflowed with hope. He leaned back in the chair, crossed his arms over his chest and smiled softly in satisfaction, still alone, but not lonely anymore.

Chapter Ten

The holiday flew by, and by midmorning Saturday Deni and Lacy were in the car, headed back home. Deni hummed softly to herself, more content than she'd been in a long time. Her parents had been great, making her feel loved and accepted. Thinking back, Deni now realized that Lacy had a lot to do with that. She looked toward her young roommate, who was searching for a country-and-western station on the radio, and smiled at her fondly.

Lacy caught her eye and smiled back. "You look different than you did on the trip up," the teenager commented. "More relaxed and very pleased about something."

Deni laughed. "That doesn't surprise me. I *am* more relaxed and I'm definitely pleased about, well, about most everything in general. And I think maybe I owe you a big vote of thanks."

Lacy raised an eyebrow in mock surprise. "Me? What did I do?"

"For one thing, you changed the subject every time my parents mentioned how much they were looking forward to the grandchildren I was going to give them someday," Deni said, remembering how cleverly Lacy had fielded their not-so-subtle suggestions that it was high time Deni settled down. They'd finally taken the hint and quit bringing up the topic.

Lacy grinned smugly. "I did, didn't I?"

"Yes, you did," Deni said, somehow keeping her face straight. "And you got them to admit that having a daughter with a dress shop in Garland, Texas, is every parent's dream come true."

Lacy shrugged. "Well, isn't it?"

Deni had to laugh. *"And,"* she continued, now smiling broadly, "you finagled a promise that they would come to see me for Christmas. I still haven't figured out how on earth you pulled that one off. They've never been out of Arkansas."

"It was simple," Lacy assured her. "Thursday night after you went to bed, the three of us had a nice long talk. Your mom asked me about Hunter and I told them everything. I also mentioned that the two of you would be having a Christmas wedding."

"What?"

"I also mentioned that—"

"How could you?" Deni raged, the car weaving slightly as her attention switched from her driving to her companion. "That's out of the question!" No wonder her parents had abandoned grandbabies as a topic of conversation. They thought she was about to get married and produce some.

Lacy put a hand on the wheel, steadying the speeding vehicle. "But a Christmas wedding would be so pretty," she argued. "I could wear that red dress you've got in the shop window, we could decorate with holly, and—"

"Lacy Beecher, have you lost your mind?" Deni exploded. "Hunter and I aren't even speaking."

"But you will be soon," Lacy argued, clearly bewildered. "You said when you'd exorcised all your ghosts you'd be willing to take on my brother—"

"Right. I did," Deni agreed. "But I've got another one or two ghosts to deal with."

"Such as?"

"A miserable marriage, a husband who made fun of my background and my dreams—"

"My brother would never do that," Lacy interjected earnestly.

Deni sighed lustily. "I know. And I guess the thought of marrying Hunter is really not so bad, but you're forgetting that by now he may have decided he doesn't need an emotional cripple in his life."

Lacy snorted at that. "Speaking of emotional cripples, my brother is going to be one soon if you don't put him out of his misery. Why don't you take the initiative and call him?"

"But he's probably still mad at me," Deni argued.

"He's not mad *at* you, silly," Lacy retorted. "He's mad *about* you. Now we're almost in Little Rock. Stop and give him a call. Please?"

"You really think I should?"

"I sure do."

"But what will I say?" Deni asked, frowning.

"Say 'Hello, Hunter, this is Deni. I love you madly and I'm on my way home.' That ought to break the ice."

Deni had to laugh. That should, indeed, break the ice, but did she dare? Their last encounter had been anything but pleasant. What if he wasn't willing to talk things out, to compromise? Panic started to well inside her but, drawing on newfound courage, she ruthlessly suppressed it, exclaiming, "All right. I'll do it."

And she did—from a pay phone at the first service station they came to. But he wasn't home. She tried him once every hour until they reached Texarkana, with similar results and increasing frustration. Finally she called Hattie only to discover that Hunter was helping out at a rodeo at the Mesquite Arena and would be gone until late.

"I knew that!" Lacy exclaimed, slapping a palm to her forehead when Deni told her. "I just forgot."

"I thought the rodeo season was over the end of September," Deni said, confused.

"It is. This is some special charity event. A lot of past champions will be there. It should really be good. I was supposed to go with Seth if we got home in time. Some friends of his will be there."

"Why didn't you tell me you had a date?" Deni asked. "We could have left Houston hours earlier. I was getting antsy anyway."

"It's not a date and it doesn't really matter if I don't get to go," Lacy assured her.

But Deni wouldn't settle for that. "What time is the rodeo?" she asked, a plan forming in her brain.

"Seven-thirty, I think. Why? Do you want to go with us?"

"Maybe. What will Hunter be doing there?"

"Well, he used to rodeo all the time—did a little of everything. I doubt that he'll compete, though. He's probably just going to help behind the chutes or something. Or maybe he's going to be a clown. He's done that before, too." Lacy slid Deni a sidelong glance, her eyes twinkling with mischief.

"A clown! My God, that's as bad as riding the bulls," Deni exploded. She pushed her foot down on the gas pedal, sending the car flying down the four-lane highway. "You bet I'll go with you two and if he's in a clown costume he'd better be damned good and disguised!"

The air at the Mesquite Arena crackled with excitement. Deni felt it the minute she stepped out of her car. She walked with Seth and Lacy to the huge, covered arena. Although they were a little late, people were still filing into the building. It was Deni's first visit and she was awed by the massive, weather-protected structure. Her eyes took in the seating, from the bleachers to the glassed-in sky boxes. She could well believe Seth's comment that the arena seated six thousand, and couldn't help but wonder how she would ever find Hunter in the crush of people now inside the arena.

They had good seats near one of the chutes. As soon as they were settled, she voiced her concerns to Seth, almost shouting to be heard above the thousands of cheering fans. Since the place was crawling with past champions who had volunteered their skills for a worthy cause, her cousin offered to slip behind the scenes to find Hunter and maybe meet a few heroes while he was at it.

When he left, Deni looked over to Lacy, who was sitting between her and a young man Seth had introduced as his new roommate. Lacy seemed as entranced by the roommate as by the activity in the arena below.

"Do I look all right?" Deni asked her, nervously straightening her hair. She was anxious to see Hunter and wanted to look her best.

Lacy dragged her eyes away from the youth beside her. "For the hundredth time, you look wonderful. That shade of blue is your color!"

"Thanks." Deni glanced down at her brightly colored western shirt, jeans and boots. She had to smile, thinking how long it had been since she had dressed like this and how surprised Hunter would be to see her.

The announcer's voice came over the air, heralding the first event—bull riding. Although Deni hated every aspect of that sport, she was relieved it would be first. She wanted to get it over with, knowing she would probably have a pretty good time once she had that particular event under her belt. Never mind that Stu and Seth had both ridden the bulls for years in spite of her very verbal disapproval—and with only minor breaks and bruises. Deni still died a thousand deaths every time they, or any other cowboy, competed.

Suddenly she and Lacy were both jostled by Seth who appeared out of nowhere to plop down beside Deni. His face was tense and Deni frowned at him, sensing something was amiss. "What's wrong? Couldn't you find him?"

"Someone pointed out his truck and horse trailer, but—"

"Horse trailer?" Lacy exclaimed, leaning forward so she could see Seth better. "Why'd he bring a horse? Surely he's not competing?"

"Actually, he—" Seth began, but his voice was lost in the blaring of the announcer's voice, which now echoed around the arena.

"And here's our first bull rider, a former Mesquite champion, Hunter Nash. Hunter is also a World Champion and made the NFR two years in a row. He graciously agreed to come here tonight to help us out. Hunter is riding Beelzebub...."

The announcer's words were drowned by the sudden ringing in Deni's ears. She couldn't breathe, couldn't speak, couldn't move for a moment. Then she leaped to her feet, afraid that she was about to witness the death of the man she loved.

"I've got to stop him," she exclaimed.

"You can't. It's too late," Seth argued.

"He's going to be killed," Deni cried, biting her lip to keep from bursting into tears from sheer terror. "Oh, God." With that, Seth got to his feet, and practically dragged her toward the exit. An agitated Lacy followed on their heels.

"Hunter has his work cut out for him tonight," the announcer continued. The crowd roared with excitement. "And they're out of the chute . . . !"

Seth tightened his grip on Deni, determined, she knew, to save her from the heartache of seeing Hunter crushed beneath the hooves of a bloodthirsty bull. But she broke free, suddenly unable to bear the suspense of that eight-second ride that always seemed like an eternity. She slipped past her cousin, running to the railing that lined the arena.

The bull twisted and turned, trying to rid himself of the determined rider that Deni loved so much. She held her breath, unaware that Seth and Lacy had joined her. Her eyes were glued to the dueling pair on the dirt floor below. Her heart thudded against her ribs as she stood, hypnotized with fear, praying for the buzzer that would signal the time limit. Just as that welcome sound filled her ears, Hunter's body shifted and he lost his equilibrium, sliding sideways off the writhing bull. To Deni's horror, his right hand was caught in the bull rope. Still attached to the beast, he was dragged several yards, his body jolted with every lurching leap.

Vainly Hunter struggled to get to his feet so that he could free his hand. The bullfighting clowns ran into the arena, distracting the animal long enough for Hunter to free himself, falling into the dirt. Apparently unhurt, he was immediately on his feet, but not out of harm's way. Beelzebub, seemingly enraged by the loss of his prey, charged the cowboy, who made a mad, stumbling dash for the safety of the railing that was a few yards away.

Deni heard the collective gasps of the crowd when Hunter tripped and fell. She saw the charging bull at his heels, the long, deadly looking horns. She screamed, covering her eyes with her hands to block the view of his certain demise.

"He's all right, Deni! He's all right!" Lacy had grabbed her hands, pulling them down so she could see Hunter scramble up over a fence and out of the arena.

Overcome with relief, Deni sagged back against Seth for a moment, sucking in big gulps of air in an effort to regain her shattered composure.

Awkwardly Seth put his arm around her, patting her shoulder. "Are you okay?"

"Yes," she murmured weakly.

"I thought he was a goner," Lacy said with a sigh, putting a hand to her heart.

"He's going to wish he was," Deni informed her coldly, turning on her heel and stomping past the rows of seats to the corridor that led behind the chutes.

"You're not supposed to go back there," Seth argued, grabbing her arm to halt her.

"You did," she retorted, never breaking stride.

"But Deni—"

She ignored him, slipping through the gate that separated competitors from fans and then winding her way through the maze of cowboys, cowgirls and horses that were everywhere. Seth and Lacy followed, but Deni didn't even notice, her eyes darting from side to side, looking for Hunter's yellow western shirt, spotted with dirt, or his hat with its rattlesnake-skin band. Deni stopped short when she spotted him a short distance away, his back to her, and then charged the remaining feet that separated them. She reached out, tapping on his shoulder to get his attention. He turned, his eyes widening in shock when he recognized her.

"Deni, honey! What are you doing here?"

"Don't you 'Deni, honey' me, Hunter Nash!" she exploded, every word punctuated by a forefinger poked into his chest. "How dare you get on that bull and risk your fool neck! Are you trying to get yourself killed? Did you ever stop to think what could happen if you—"

His lips smothered her tirade; his hug squeezed the breath from her lungs. Lost in his hungry kiss, Deni almost forgot her fury—almost. With effort, she mustered enough wits to wedge her arms between them, trying to push him away.

"Let me go! I'm furious with you and—"

He kissed her again. Deni stiffened, telling herself she should resist, but the touch of his lips was pure magic, melting her resolve and she promptly forgot what she had wanted to say.

He raised his head several thudding heartbeats later, clearly as addled as she was. "I didn't mean to scare you, honey. I don't usually make such a mess of a ride. I wonder if someone's trying to tell me it's time to hang up my spurs."

"Someone sure is," she scolded, finally managing to put several inches between them. "And I'm also here to tell you if you ever ride another bull you'd damn well better hope he kills you, because if he doesn't, *I will*."

Hunter laughed and reached for her. "Yes, ma'am."

Deni sidestepped him. "I'm serious. There'll be no December wedding unless you promise you won't ever do that again."

She watched the words sink in, heard him catch his breath and then blurt out, "I promise."

Still holding him at arm's length, Deni cocked her head, trying to gauge his sincerity. "Do you mean it?"

"I mean it. I mean it," he earnestly assured her. "And you've got to promise me something, too."

"What's that?" Deni asked, though she suspected she knew the answer. He was going to ask her not to go to New York. And what would she say? she wondered, her eyes drinking in the sight of the beloved man before her—a man so crucial to her happiness. Deni suddenly acknowledged that he was much more important than any design school and she could wait a while to go away—wait until a time when he was secure in their love. She never doubted for a moment that day would come, a realization that told her she was finally ready to take on the challenge of Hunter Nash. Her heart sang with delight.

"Promise me that if someone in New York offers you the most exciting job in the world, one you'd be crazy to turn down, you'll come back and get me."

Deni's jaw dropped in astonishment. "You'd live with me in New York?"

"If that's what it took to keep you."

Tears of gratitude and relief filled her eyes, blurring his face. "But I don't want a job up north. Everything I love is here."

He framed her face with his hands, gently brushing away an errant tear with his thumb. "Here?"

"*Right* here," she assured him, raising her heels so she could place a kiss on his chin. He dipped his head, intercepting that kiss with his lips. Deni pressed her body against his, putting all her love into the embrace and then jumping in surprise when the sound of cheers and applause intruded their joy. They both looked around, startled to discover they were the center attraction in a ring of very interested bystanders, two of whom were Seth and Lacy—both grinning. Deni's face flamed and she tried to break free but, laughing, Hunter wouldn't let her.

"Are you competing in any other events?" Deni demanded, highly flustered.

"I'd planned to, but I think maybe that one was enough for this ol' cowpoke after all."

"Then let's go. We need to talk."

"Can we go, too?" Lacy asked eagerly, her face beaming with excitement.

"Nope," Hunter told her. "We want to be alone. You and Seth stay here."

"But this was just getting good," Lacy argued, with an exaggerated pout.

Seth took her arm, bending down to whisper something in her ear. Lacy put her hand over her mouth, muttering, "Oops. I'd forgotten about him." She placed a quick kiss on her brother's cheek, hugged Deni hard and headed back to the stands, with Seth right behind.

"Forgot who?" Hunter asked Deni, frowning, a watchful eye on his sister, who was hurrying away.

"Never mind," Deni told him, noting with relief that most of the bystanders had begun to drift back to the excitement in the arena. "Let's get out of here."

It was quite dark by the time they got Hunter's horse loaded into the trailer and had crawled into the cab of the truck. Hunter reached to start the ignition, but halted sitting back instead. He stared out the windshield at nothing, strangely silent for a moment.

"What's wrong?" Deni asked, sliding across the seat to slip her arm through his and lay her head on his shoulder.

"I was just thinking how lucky I am to have found a woman who loves me enough to see what I want to be instead of what I am." He smiled at her tenderly. "That picture you drew of me meant more than you'll ever know."

Deni sat bolt upright, frowning at him through the dark. "You saw that?"

"But of course I did," he told her. "You mailed it to me."

"I mailed it to you?"

"Uh-huh." When she didn't immediately respond to that, he prompted, "I got it Friday."

Suddenly realizing just how that must have come about, Deni shook her head. "As much as I hate to admit this, I have to tell you I gave that drawing to Lacy. *She* must have mailed it to you."

He digested that in silence. "So what you wrote across the top was meant for her."

"Yes," Deni said. "She told me exactly what to say, probably intending to send it to you all along."

Hunter laughed softly. "That little sister of mine is pretty devious, isn't she?"

"Darned devious," Deni qualified. "She's invited my parents to Texas for a Christmas wedding."

"No kidding?"

"No kidding. That really puts us on the spot, you know. I'd hate to disappoint them."

"Why do that? You know I'm all for the idea. I suggested the same thing days ago."

Deni smiled. "So you did, and a Christmas wedding sounds perfect, but I think I should warn you that Lacy is planning on wearing that red dress in the shop window."

Hunter groaned. "But that dress is too revealing."

"She looks great in it," Deni assured him saucily, adding, "and I'll even give you a family discount, as if you needed one!"

"You know, the word 'family' has a damned nice ring to it," Hunter said. He gave her a long look and then wrapped his arms around her, claiming her lips. When he would have pulled away, Deni tightened the embrace, trailing her lips across his cheek and chin and tracing lazy circles over his back with her fingertips. Hunter moaned softly in response. "Unless you want to start that family right here, I suggest you stop."

"Right," she murmured against his collarbone, but she didn't move her hands.

"I mean it," he cautioned huskily. Deni sighed and released him. Hunter reached for the key, but hesitated again. "Deni, I think I should warn you that marriage to me won't be any bed of roses and even though I'm resigned to your going off to that school of yours, I'll probably give you hell when departure time rolls around."

"And I'll probably get all defensive and we'll fight again."

"Almost certainly."

There was a thoughtful silence and then Deni murmured, "I've always heard how much fun it is to make up. Maybe we'll find out."

"There's no maybe to it," Hunter responded. "We *will* make up. I won't settle for less." He took a deep breath and then plunged ahead. "There's also the matter of my little sister. She may want to live at the ranch while she goes to college. How do you feel about that?''

"I don't mind at all," Deni assured him.

Once again, Hunter reached out to start the engine, this time actually doing it. Before he put the truck in gear, however, he turned to her. "There's just one more thing I need to clear up."

"What's that?" Deni asked, snuggling against him.

"If you'd known I was going to end up with that picture, what would you have written on it?"

Deni made a great show of making up her mind, rubbing her chin, frowning thoughtfully. Then she leaned toward him, impishly whispering into his ear a sentiment that made his breath leave his lungs in a slow whoosh of anticipation.

"All right!" he exploded, stripping the gears in his haste to put the truck in motion. Then he peeled out of the parking lot, leaving behind a cloud of dust as they headed for their happily ever after.

*   *   *   *   *

NAVY BLUES
Debbie Macomber

Between the devil and the deep blue sea . . .

At Christmastime, Lieutenant Commander Steve Kyle finds his heart
anchored by the past, so he vows to give his ex-wife wide berth. But
Carol Kyle is quaffing milk and knitting tiny pastel blankets with a
vengeance. She's determined to have a baby, and only one man will
do as father-to-be—the only man she's ever loved . . . her own
bullheaded ex-husband!

You met Steve and Carol in NAVY WIFE (Special Edition #494)—
you'll cheer for them in NAVY BLUES (Special Edition #518). (And
as a bonus for NAVY WIFE fans, newlyweds Rush and Lindy Cal-
laghan reveal a surprise of their own. . . .)

Each book stands alone—together they're Debbie Macomber's most
delightful duo to date! Don't miss

NAVY BLUES
Available in April,
only in *Silhouette Special Edition*.
Having the "blues" was never
so much fun!